She Gets July

ISBN: 978-1-947079-25-0

She Gets July

By Susan Page Davis

Chapter I

Rebecca froze when she spotted a postcard nestled innocuously between the phone bill and an L.L. Bean catalog. An eagerness she would have denied made her fingers shake as she picked it out of the day's handful of mail, and she read it with bittersweet satisfaction. Rob was faithful, even though she had released him from all commitment three years ago.

Dear Rebecca, I've checked things out and turned on the water and electricity. Any time you want to use the cottage, it's ready for you. RW

She stared at the neat, backward-slanted printing he had developed in grammar school, and tears came to her eyes. She dropped the postcard to the table and went to her bedroom to change out of her nursing uniform, determined to put Rob Wallace out of her mind.

She fixed herself a sketchy supper and carried it to the living room, where she ate it while watching the local news. When she took her dishes to the sink, she realized she was avoiding the table because she didn't want to see the postcard again, and she didn't want to think about Rob.

But the cottage was still an important part of her life, even if Rob wasn't. She picked up the card and flipped it over to examine the address side. It was the plain manila card sold in the post office, not the scenic kind, with lovely Maine vistas enticing you to get away for the weekend in Vacationland.

That was just what she would do. The cottage was hers for the rest of May, and she would go up this weekend. The ice had barely gone out of the lake, and the water would still be too cold for swimming, but she could sit on the dock in the late spring sun and have a fire in the stone fireplace in the chilly evenings. And she could get out and walk for miles on the dirt roads near the lake, satisfying her latent longings for the country.

Of course, there would be reminders of Rob everywhere. She didn't need any photos to see him, even after all this time. In her mind's eye, he was there, bent over the postcard with the pen in his left hand, frowning in concentration over the address, his brown eyes placid and his chestnut hair fluffy and tousled.

Her eyes stung, and she blinked hard. It was worth the painful memories, to get away from Portland for a couple of days and blow the cobwebs from her brain.

She wavered, looking down again at the words he had written—when? Yesterday? The day before? The postmark said May 4. Saturday, two days ago.

She hadn't seen him in more than three years. They'd talked on the phone a couple of times, briefly. It was business only, to tie up loose ends concerning the cottage. He never tried to see her when she drove an hour to the north to use it. But the postcards had come every spring. *Rebecca, the cottage is ready.*

Rob sat at his computer, fine-tuning an elevation for a new elementary school. In a few more hours, he'd be done with the project, but he didn't really want to be finished. Between projects, his mind drifted too much, and he didn't want that right now.

He'd been out to the cottage Saturday, to check on things and make sure it was ready for Rebecca. It was May, and she'd be going there soon. May was hers, then he would move to the lake for a month.

On the last day of June, he would pack up all his things and move from the lakeside, back to his parents' home, so she could

6

claim the cottage for the month of July. And on the first day of August, he would move back to the lake. It happened every year. People thought it was strange. Fine, let them think that.

His phone rang, and he picked it up.

"Hi, honey. Ready for lunch?"

Rob winced, but he was too polite to tell Brittany how uncomfortable her syrupy greeting made him. "Uh, sure. I'll meet you downstairs in a couple of minutes." He saved the computer file and stood.

"The princess beckons?" Eric, at the next desk, was a good friend, but he enjoyed needling Rob. "The chains of slavery are tightening."

Rob scowled at him. "What do you suppose your wife would say if she heard you talking like that?"

Eric grinned. "Leah would say, 'That's right. Eric's been my slave for seven years.' And she'd be right."

"You've only been married five." Rob reached for his jacket.

"Trust me, friend, it starts long before the wedding. Look at you, scrambling every day at noon."

"Twice a week," Rob said. "I told her I can't do lunch more than that."

"Oh, so you're in control, not Brittany. I'll bet you're Johnny-on-the-spot Friday nights, too. Next thing you know, she'll have you picking her up for work every day, even though it's miles out of your way. You might as well marry her now."

That hit home. Brittany had suggested he pick her up in the morning, but Rob had begged off. He shrugged. "Hey, it's not that serious."

Eric nodded doubtfully. "Right. You've been dating how long?"

"Just a couple of months."

"Mm-hmm. Two months."

"Or three. I forget."

"Tell me she hasn't been hinting for a diamond."

Rob frowned. "It's pretty early for that, don't you think?"

"So? Talk isn't enough for a woman like Brittany. If you don't cough up a tangible token of your adoration—preferably a ring—pretty soon, she'll make you miserable."

"Did Leah do that to you?"

"Well, no, but Leah's nothing like Brittany. Not her type at all."

Rob headed for the elevator shaking his head. He wasn't ready to make things exclusive with Brittany, let alone permanent, but he wasn't about to admit it when Eric was implying that marriage was a deathtrap. Eric made no secret of his opinion that Brittany was the wrong choice for Rob, and he couldn't resist ribbing him every chance he got.

Maybe Eric was right. Brittany was a bit of a clinging vine. She definitely wanted to move things along faster than Rob did. If Eric wasn't so cynical, maybe Rob could talk to him seriously about the relationship. But he knew what Eric would say. *Run, do not walk.*

❧❧❧

With warmer weather, people in the city were getting outside, gardening, biking, traveling, exercising. And having more accidents. When Rebecca arrived at Ainsley Hospital's emergency room that morning, she was immediately handed the chart of a burn patient. She did her best to make the screaming little boy comfortable and soothe his frightened mother.

"I can't believe this happened." Mrs. Leeds wiped distractedly at the tears rolling down her face. "I had no idea Kenny could reach the coffee maker. He got hold of the cord and pulled it over on himself."

"It's going to be all right," Rebecca assured her. She stayed with them while the doctor examined the boy and ordered pain medication. She brought the painkiller and the supplies she would need to dress the wound.

Mrs. Leeds grew pale as the doctor cut the dead skin away, revealing the depth of the burned tissue.

"Maybe you should wait outside," Rebecca said gently.

"No, I want to stay with him." The boy's mother kept one hand on his head. His screams wound down to moans as the medication took effect.

"Will he be admitted?" She gazed anxiously at the doctor.

"No, you'll be able to take him home. We'll give you instructions on how to watch for infection and change the dressing. Don't let him get the dressing wet."

"Will he have a scar?"

"Time will tell. Bring him back tomorrow. I'll be here from seven to seven."

Mrs. Leeds nodded at the doctor's noncommittal answer, dashing away tears. "Thank God it didn't hit him in the face."

When at last Kenny and his mother headed out the door, Rebecca shook her head, positive the poor little fellow would end up with a lot of scarring on his burned arm. She finished charting the procedures and supplies used on the boy, then went to the chart rack for the paperwork on her next patient.

Rebecca was good at her stressful job. She could calm most people but remain objective. Long ago, she'd learned to overlook the unpleasant sights and smells of the ER. All too often, terror and anger erupted, and she tried to calm the patients. For much of her shift, she concentrated on reducing the anxiety of the hurting people and their families.

Today was extra crazy. Following a pileup on the interstate during the morning rush hour, four victims arrived. They kept the staff busy most of the morning. Things had barely quieted down before a couple rushed in with a toddler who had fallen into a Jacuzzi, and EMTs wheeled in an elderly woman suffering a heart attack. Between critical patients, Rebecca handled the usual assortment of fractures, cuts and bruises, chest pain, and sudden illness.

Her best friend, Faye Roman, worked the registration desk, which was separated from the ER waiting room by a glass partition. Rebecca took her last chart of the morning and sat down at the station nearest Faye's, hoping a lull would come and they could make plans for lunch together.

Faye sat facing a young mother who held a sobbing two-year-old girl. The mother alternately tried to quiet the little girl and keep an eye on her four-year-old son. He kept wandering into the waiting room, to stare at the people sitting there.

The mom would answer one of Faye's questions, then jump up, calling, "Anthony! You come back here!" That inevitably set off Anthony's sister into ear-splitting howls. Rebecca tried to shut them out as she worked, and wished she had sat beyond the divider, where the noise still penetrated but was less distracting.

"You know what?" Faye asked the mother after the fifth interruption, "I think I'll send you down to Express Care. We're really busy this morning, and it will be an hour before Carissa sees a doctor if you stay here. But at Express Care they should get you in and out fairly quickly."

"You mean this isn't a real emergency, is that it?" The woman's lip curled. "She's got a temp of a hundred and one, for crying out loud."

"Yes, but I think she'll see a doctor quicker over there. She might just need some medication, and they can get you that faster. You'll get care every bit as good, but you won't have to wait as long. We have to take critical patients first here."

The mother sighed. "Okay, so what do I—Anthony! Come back here!"

Carissa began to scream again, and Rebecca bent over her clipboard, trying to focus as Faye pulled a sheet of paper from the printer and thrust it into the mother's hand. "Follow the green arrows on the floor. Express Care. Trust me, they'll help you there. I'll call and tell them you're on the way."

Five more patients waited in line beyond Faye's cubicle. Rebecca realized that lunch with Faye was a lost cause. She would have to scramble if she wanted to get even a quick bite.

"Your name, please," Faye said to her next patient. The husky man in blue work clothes sat down in the booth opposite her. He held his left forearm with his right hand. "Have you been a patient here in the last year, Mr. Leary?"

"Yes. Last fall."

"What's the problem today?"

"I think my wrist is broken."

Rebecca glanced up from her work. Faye was studying the chart on her computer screen, but Rebecca could see that the man's face was pale.

"A doctor will see you as soon as possible," Faye said. "Just let me ask you a few questions. Did someone bring you in?"

"No, I drove myself."

Faye raised her eyebrows. "Is your insurance the same as it was before?"

"Yes, I—" He sucked in a deep breath, and Faye looked at him sharply. "I don't feel so good," he said.

Rebecca stood as Faye lurched to her feet. She saw then that blood oozed between Leary's fingers.

"Rebecca," Faye yelled, but she was already at the man's side.

"We need help," Rebecca called toward the triage desk.

Kelly, the triage nurse, hurried into the reception area. Rebecca managed to keep Leary from slumping to the floor while Kelly rushed to get a wheelchair. They got him into it and through the doors into one of the exam rooms.

"I need help now," Rebecca yelled, and the doctor on call came swiftly. After Kelly helped transfer Leary to a gurney, she waited with him. He lay alternately apologizing and cursing as the doctor examined his injury. The minutes crawled until his medication took effect. Rebecca stuck with him while he was sent to X-ray and back. By the time an aide wheeled him off to surgery, his eyelids were drooping.

Lunch didn't come her way until almost one thirty, and by the time her shift ended at three she was exhausted. She stayed an extra twenty minutes to clean up an exam room and complete her paperwork. Faye was on duty until five. Rebecca waved to her and walked alone out the nearest exit and across the vast parking lot, pulling in deep breaths of cool air.

The lakeside cottage was looking good. Three more days of this, and she could get away. Solitude and tranquility beckoned as she drove home.

Her apartment was one of four in an eighty-year-old house, in a declining residential neighborhood. The city had approved construction of a convenience store almost directly across from Rebecca's building, and the grinding noise of heavy equipment throbbed in the air as she unlocked her door.

Suddenly she longed for the lake so desperately that she could almost taste the morning breeze off the water. The large trees between the cottage and the lake would be leafing out, and she could sit on the dock in a lounge chair, sipping hot tea. The cottage had no phone. No patients. No television, no time clock, no supervisors, and no cement mixers.

The drive to the cottage would take her through Belgrade, past the old house where her family had lived for twenty years. It would bring out agonizing memories of sweet interludes with Rob. But, yes, it would definitely be worth it.

Maybe she could recapture the old serenity. The peace. It seemed like a long time since she'd had that. She thought she knew the main cause.

She used to pray for her patients silently as she filled out their charts. When had she stopped doing that? Even at home, she rarely read her Bible anymore, or spent time in prayer. She was always too tired at night, too rushed in the morning.

Yes, she determined as she pulled the mail from the box, she would go to the lake, and the first thing she would pack was her Bible. Lately, whenever she thought about the battered Bible lying on her nightstand, it brought her guilt instead of joy. Time to change that.

She opened the refrigerator and scanned its meager contents. Nothing good. She closed the door and sat down at the table.

Reviewing her day, she realized that the only time she had thought about God was when little Kenny's mother said, "Thank God it didn't hit him in the face."

Father, I do thank you that Kenny's burn wasn't worse. Please keep his pain away tonight, and give his mother rest.

Rebecca was sorry she hadn't offered spiritual support to that woman in the emergency room. She couldn't speak aloud

12

of her faith to patients unless they initiated the conversation, but she still could have prayed silently on the spot. It hadn't occurred to her at the time.

She had to admit that her spiritual apathy began when she and Rob broke up, when she had felt so hurt, so betrayed, so alone. Since then, she had become independent, self-sufficient and a little bit tough. *When I let Rob go, I let You go,* she confessed to God. *Please, Lord, I don't want to go the rest of my life estranged from You, too. Show me the way back.*

Chapter 2

Brittany was waiting in the lobby when Rob stepped off the elevator. He had thought she was beautiful the first time he saw her. Now he had revised that assessment. She was perhaps a bit more than conventionally pretty, her fine blond hair falling in soft waves to her shoulders, her blue eyes rimmed in darker lines. Her loveliness seemed skillfully manufactured.

She stepped toward him and raised her cheek a little, and he knew she expected him to kiss her. He felt his face flush. Did he really want to be routinely kissing Brittany in public? Instead, he pulled out a smile he didn't feel. "Hi."

Yep, she was definitely disappointed, but he wasn't going to start kissing her in his employer's lobby.

"Hi, sweetie. Where are we going?" she asked, smoothing the short navy skirt of her suit.

Rob hustled her toward the door, away from the receptionist's desk. "I don't know, something quick. I'm in the middle of the Harmony school project." He should have just told her he was too busy to go out for lunch. She had come to expect it, though. He'd taken her out a couple of times in the early spring, and now she wanted to make it a weekly date, besides coaxing him into extra luncheons together.

"How about that new place across the park?" she asked.

"Fine." They walked across the green, past the cannon and a carved stone bench. The emerald grass was crowding out the last signs of the dead brown winter thatch. Around the war monument, daffodils and narcissus were blooming, and the pigeons were out in force. Rob usually felt anticipation this time of year, but it hadn't come when he'd turned the calendar to May this time.

He didn't say much during the meal, and Brittany grew less patient with him as the minutes ticked by.

"Is anything wrong?" she asked at last.

He sighed and sat back. He had eaten only half his food, but he wasn't hungry. "No, I'm just stressed with this school thing."

She smiled in sympathy. "Deadline creeping up on you?"

"Yes, but we'll be on schedule. It's just the last-minute changes that aggravate me."

"Well, pretty soon you'll be moving to that little cottage on the lake. You'll be able to unwind."

"I hope so."

"I thought the project was going well."

She seemed genuinely concerned about him, and Rob felt a pang of remorse. It wasn't only the assignment that was draining him.

"It's fine. We'll be finished by the end of the week. I'm just ... tired, I guess."

"Why don't we do something relaxing this weekend? Do you want to go to the coast? We could drive to Pemaquid."

"No, I don't think so."

"Say, why don't you show me the cottage?" She sat forward eagerly, her eyes gleaming. He tried to believe she had just thought of it and hadn't been waiting to spring the suggestion. "You told me it's quiet and restful. It sounds so idyllic. We could take a picnic Saturday and get away, where you don't have to think about clients. Nice and quiet, just you and me."

He shook his head. "I told you, I'm not the sole owner."

"You mean ..." she eyed him speculatively. "Someone else is there now? It's awfully early."

Rob picked up his coffee mug and took a sip, then set it down deliberately. "I have June and August. The other owner has May, July, and September."

16

"My goodness, nobody gets April and October?" She smiled coyly, but there was granite beneath her words. She turned sideways in her chair and crossed her legs, revealing a length of smooth thigh that was hard to ignore.

Rob deliberately didn't look at her or the man at the next table, who was sneaking glances at Brittany. "If I wanted to stay there in October, I could. Do some bird hunting, maybe."

"And he gets November, for deer season." She watched his face intently.

"I'd better get back to the office." Rob pulled out his wallet.

She waited until they were halfway across the park. "Rob, don't you think you should tell me everything?"

He was silent, groping for a clue to her thoughts, but he couldn't quite follow her. Why did she think he was obligated to share his private concerns with her? He honestly hadn't led her on.

"Because you told me you've never been married before, honey, but this seems too much like—"

He stopped a few yards from the cannon and faced her grimly. "Like what?"

"Sorry, but this cottage thing just seems like a divorce settlement or something. Joint custody, or tenancy, or whatever you call it."

A huge emptiness opened wider and wider inside him. He liked Brittany, he really did. She had a way of making him feel wanted and liked. When she was at her best, she also made him feel competent and strong. But at other times she made him feel worthless.

She wasn't the type of woman he had always imagined committing himself to, and he had let things go too far. He could see that now. Even though he hadn't made any sort of commitment, she assumed he was hers. He had mentioned the cottage to her so she would be prepared when he changed his residence for a few weeks, but he'd tried to avoid giving the details of the arrangement.

The curiosity it sparked in her brought out a disagreeable, prying side of Brittany he had never seen. It was too much like

17

the scenario Eric had painted, and Rob didn't like the uncertainty that plagued him, or the regret he couldn't shake whenever he thought about the cottage.

"Look, there's no divorce. I told you, I've never been married. I wouldn't lie to you." He swallowed and looked away. She didn't know him well enough, that was all. But did he really want her to know him better?

Her eyes held a calculating glitter. She wasn't satisfied, he could see that.

"Can I see the cottage?"

"Maybe sometime. Not now." He turned and walked toward the office, and Brittany kept pace in silence.

Rebecca put her key in the lock and turned it slowly. Stepping over the cottage's threshold in May was always difficult. She held her breath and went in, stopping as the memories deluged her.

They had been so happy, so excited, when they found the snug little two-bedroom cottage. Rob dreamed of building a lakeside home, but they knew it would be a while before they could afford a real house on the waterfront. This summer cottage was ideal for them.

Rebecca had finished nursing school and been working for a year, saving her money. Rob, facing his second year of graduate school, had come into a small legacy from his grandfather. They had split the down payment, calling it their wedding present to each other.

They would be married the next June and spend all summer on the lake. Their children would grow up here, learning to swim like little fish before they could walk. They'd have long, lazy weekends and breathtaking sunsets together. And in winter, they could rent an apartment in town. Maybe later, when Rob was established as an architect, they could build a bigger, year-round home on the water.

She shivered. The cottage had been closed up all winter, and a musty smell of old varnish and cedar shingles lingered in the chilly air. Rebecca dropped her canvas bag in the kitchen and went quickly into the living room, which was dominated by the fieldstone fireplace. Rob had left her a good supply of firewood and laid a fire in the hearth for her.

With a trembling hand, she reached up to the mantel and took a match. The birch bark and paper caught immediately, and she sat down, pulling her long cardigan close around her as she watched the blaze grow, snapping and popping as it devoured the evidence of his thoughtfulness.

It wasn't supposed to be like this. Rob should be here with her, holding her close until the cottage warmed, spinning dreams with her.

Chapter 3

After supper Wednesday evening, Rob rose and picked up his own dishes and his dad's. "I'll load the dishwasher, Mom. You go ahead."

She hesitated a moment, but she didn't ask if he was going to the mid-week Bible study with them. Rob hadn't gone to church on Wednesday nights for a long time.

"All right. Thank you." She left the kitchen to change her clothes.

By the time his parents were ready to head out, the dishwasher was running and Rob was wiping down the counters.

His dad paused in the doorway. "'Bye, son."

"See you later," Rob said.

He finished up the kitchen chores and went up to his room and kicked off his shoes. Lying down on his bed, he reached for the crime novel on his nightstand. He'd hardly read a page before laying it down spine up on his chest.

Brittany's questions about the cottage still bothered him. He felt slightly guilty for holding back from her, but another part of his brain told him that was foolish. He had a right to his privacy. They weren't engaged. He hadn't even asked her to limit her dating to him.

Of course, she would probably think he was naïve if she knew he had only dated one other girl more than once before he met her. Maybe that was why he found it so hard to judge her moods—he just didn't have a lot of experience with women. The ones he knew best—his mother, his sister Debbie, and yes, even Rebecca—were open and easy to read. With Brittany, he was never sure he knew what she was thinking or why.

In February, shortly after she'd come to work at Hanson Associates, he'd noticed her and thought she was fascinating. She had a confident polish and independence that he cautiously admired. And she was more than middle-of-the-road attractive, on the alluring side.

She worked in the finance department, doing estimates for the firm's bids on new projects. Rob had written her off as out of his league. Then, around the middle of March, she'd taken him by surprise when she struck up a conversation with him in the elevator. After that, she seemed to make a point of being around whenever he left the building for lunch. Next thing he knew, they'd scheduled a date to a concert—at her suggestion.

He'd been flattered and figured it wouldn't last. She'd get bored and move on to someone more sophisticated. But she hadn't. She seemed to genuinely like his company, and a couple of weeks later, still unsettled as to whether or not he really wanted to become involved with a woman again, he'd asked her out a second time.

Now they were perceived in the office as a couple. He had managed to keep the physical side of the relationship low key, although he sensed that Brittany wouldn't be against accelerating things. At every possible moment, she reached for his hand or sat closer than was comfortable for him. She had initiated their first kiss, and he always seemed to be the one to break the good-night embrace.

Rob liked her. Most of the time. She was smart, and she understood the finer points of his work. But he couldn't relax with her. She never made him feel comfortable the way Rebecca had. Rebecca fit like an old shoe, his mom would say. He scowled. He had to quit thinking about Rebecca. It was over.

Brittany had met his parents, but only through his machinations, when he took her to a play at the Opera House in early April. He and his sister had bought tickets for his mom and dad as an anniversary gift. They didn't sit with him and Brittany, but he'd taken her out into the lobby during the intermission and introduced her. His mother had invited Brittany to join the family for supper a week later, but she had declined, and she'd never accepted another invitation to a family event.

"Bring her to church," was his mother's standard suggestion.

As if that would happen.

Rob sat up slowly and put the book on the nightstand. Brittany and church didn't mix. She was frank about that. Rob tried not to let it factor into his feelings for her. At first it had bothered him a lot. He didn't want to get close to a woman who wasn't a believer.

But lately he'd found it tedious himself to get up on Sunday morning and go with his parents. He usually skipped Sunday evening and Wednesday night now, using work the next morning as an excuse. He needed his sleep.

For months he'd avoided the subject. He kept going once a week, so he hadn't forsaken public worship. And there was no commandment in the Bible that said you had to go to church three times a week.

He got up and walked to the open window. A cool breeze wafted through the screen, and he lowered the sash a few inches. He didn't like worrying his parents. He tried to stay cheerful around them, but it was hard to be upbeat and evasive at the same time.

The trouble was, they could sense his ambivalence about his relationship with Brittany. He supposed he should have asked himself the questions he was asking now, before he ever took her to that first concert at Colby College.

Was it just that the novelty had worn off? His pulse didn't hammer anymore when she smiled at him. The glint of her glamour had faded with daily exposure, but it was more than that. His greatest disappointment had nothing to do with externals. Eric's constant criticism hadn't helped, but Rob had to admit that Brittany was not the ideal woman he had imagined her to be when he'd first met her.

Had Brittany changed? Or had he? Had he begun to compare her to the only woman he had ever really loved? If that were true, he wasn't being fair to Brittany. She deserved a chance to be herself, without him constantly wishing her to be someone else.

The beam of headlights swept over the house as a car turned in at the driveway. It was too early for the folks to be home. He squinted out into the dusk. Debbie got out of her red Toyota and opened the trunk.

Rob went quickly down the stairs and out the door, meeting his sister on the paved driveway.

"Hey, Deb, I didn't know you were coming down."

"Neither did I." She handed him a duffel bag. "Can you take that in? I'll get the rest."

"What's up?" He set the duffel bag down inside the kitchen door.

Debbie came in behind him and set her laptop case on the table. "I wish I knew," she said grimly.

Rob faced her in surprise and caught his breath. A purple bruise surrounded Debbie's left eye. Her cheek was red and swollen. "That looks painful," he said. "What happened?"

Debbie looked away, then back at her brother. "I needed a break. I figured you and Mom and Dad wouldn't mind having me here for a day or two."

"Sure. Have you eaten?" She shook her head, and Rob turned to the refrigerator, trying to act normal. "There's some leftover chicken, and rice and squash. How does that sound?"

"Heavenly." Debbie took off her windbreaker and hung it on a hook near the back door. "I was going to stop at a fast food place, but I didn't want to take time."

"No problem." Rob took a plate from the cupboard and began filling it with leftovers, wanting to ask a million more questions.

Debbie's wedding was scheduled for the end of August. She'd worked as a researcher for a medical consortium in

Bangor, an hour to the north, for the past year, and she had an apartment in the city. She had met her fiancé, Mark Elliott, through a coworker, and things had moved quickly. They had announced the engagement the second time she brought Mark down to Belgrade, just six weeks after they met.

Debbie took the ironstone plate and slid it into the microwave. "Mom will probably have fits." She dashed a tear from her cheek with the back of her hand and winced.

"Want some ice?" Rob asked.

"It might help."

"Sit down." He worked methodically, putting ice cubes in a plastic zipper bag and wrapping it in a clean dishcloth. The microwave bell rang, and Debbie took the plate out.

"Here you go." Rob handed her the ice pack, and she held it to her cheek with her left hand while eating with her right. Rob watched her, his heart aching, but sensing she'd rather not discuss it yet. He started a pot of decaffeinated coffee and got out bowls for ice cream.

They were upstairs making up the bed in Debbie's old room when their parents drove in. Rob left Debbie to put on the pillowcases and jogged down the stairs as Connie and Stewart Wallace came through the door.

"Rob, is Debbie here?" his mother asked, looking up at him eagerly. "Her car's out front."

"Yeah, she pulled in about half an hour ago. She's upstairs."

"Is anything wrong?"

"Well—"

"Is Mark with her?" his father asked.

"No, just Deb. I haven't got the details yet, but she'd like to stay here for a few days."

"What's wrong?" His mother's brow creased with worry.

"She hasn't told me yet." A door closed upstairs, and Debbie's footsteps crossed the hall. He said hastily, "Look, Mom, this may be a little shocking, but Debbie's been hurt."

"What do you mean? Did she have an accident?"

"Oh, no," his dad said softly as Debbie came down the stairs. He strode toward her, his arms wide. "Baby, what happened?"

Connie gasped and followed her husband. Debbie collapsed in her father's arms, sobbing uncontrollably.

"Daddy, I'm sorry. I shouldn't have come here, but I didn't know what else to do. I was scared."

"Shh," said Stewart, engulfing her in his embrace. "It's all right, baby. You can stay here as long as you want."

Debbie raised her head and looked at her mother. "Mom—"

Connie stepped forward and put her arms around her daughter. "Dad's right. You can stay here. That's not a problem. Oh, honey, what happened?"

"Come sit down." Stewart tugged Connie's sleeve and guided her and Debbie toward the sofa.

"I've got coffee brewing," Rob said.

He entered the living room a few minutes later with four steaming mugs and a bottle of creamer on a tray. His parents had removed their coats, and Debbie sat between them on the sofa.

"I don't know what's gotten into Mark," Debbie choked, wiping her eyes with a tissue. "He's been so moody lately, but I never expected this."

"Is this the first time?" Stewart's face was dark with anger.

"What? You mean—"

"I mean, has he ever struck you before?"

Debbie hung her head. "Once. Last month. It wasn't this bad." She looked up at him and reached out to touch his arm beseechingly. "Dad, he didn't mean it. But I told him then that if he ever hit me again—" She broke off with a sob. "Well, here I am."

"You should have gone to the hospital," Connie said.

"No, I—I couldn't, Mom. I mean, it's just a bruise. I know it looks awful."

"Any other bruises we can't see?" her father asked.

Debbie shook her head. "I yelled and told him to leave me alone, and he—he got in his truck and drove off. I was scared to stay at the apartment. Probably he's trying to call me now and is sorry he did it, but I turned my cell phone off. I didn't dare to stick around there." Her lip quivered as she glanced up at her father.

Rob thought she was trying unsuccessfully to look brave. Her expression crumpled as her fear won out.

"I mean, what if he came back and he was still mad?"

"There, honey," Connie murmured, reaching out to hug Debbie again.

Stewart stood and paced to the front window, clearly baffled at the behavior of his daughter's fiancé. "What set him off?"

Big tears oozed out from between Debbie's eyelids. "Nothing big. We've disagreed a lot lately, about the wedding arrangements and where we're going to live after, and all kinds of things. It seems like I can't do anything right anymore."

Connie rubbed her shoulders and said nothing.

"Let's pray about this," Stewart said.

Debbie nodded, and he sat down beside her on the couch. While their father prayed for wisdom and a resolution to the conflict, Rob sat with his eyes open. A heavy weight had settled on his chest. His sister didn't deserve this. The family ought to be able to protect her somehow.

Debbie wept silently during her father's brief prayer, and Connie sniffed. They all sat in brooding silence for a moment after Stewart's *amen.*

"Do you think I should try to call him?" Debbie's voice was a hesitant squeak, and she seemed uncertain, but hopeful.

Stewart reached for a mug of coffee. "He'll come looking for you after he cools off. Why don't you take some aspirin and go to bed? We'll see how things look in the morning."

Debbie nodded slowly. "All right. What if he calls?"

"I'll talk to him," her father said.

"He hasn't been drinking, has he?" Connie asked.

"No, Mom."

"Just asking."

Debbie looked plaintively at each of them. "He's a good worker, and he's smart. He cares about me."

"Don't defend him now." There was a dangerous edge to Stewart's voice.

"I'm sorry." Tears splashed onto the knees of Debbie's jeans.

"What about work tomorrow?" her mother asked.

"I brought my laptop and a flash drive and some research files. I can call the office in the morning and ask if they'll let me work at home. Sometimes I do that. If you don't mind—"

"You can use my desk while I'm at work tomorrow," Rob said quickly.

"Thank you." Debbie stood and kissed her parents.

"You'll need sheets," Connie said wearily.

"All taken care of." Debbie tried to lighten the mood with her usual sunny smile, but it veered into a grimace.

Stewart stood and squeezed her shoulders. "Get some sleep."

"I'll take your luggage up," Rob offered.

He hauled the oversized duffel bag up the stairs. Even if Debbie had left in a hurry, she had managed to load her bag heavily.

"You got everything you need?" he asked at her doorway.

"I'll be fine." Debbie gazed up at him. "Rob, I'm sorry. I feel like I've let you all down."

"It's not your fault."

"How do you know?"

"Oh, come on."

"No, really. How do you know I didn't do something that made him really, really mad?"

"Did you?"

She looked past him, toward the stairs. "I keep asking myself that. I mean, I know we disagree on—on the timetable for things, but—" She shook her head helplessly, and the tears streamed unhindered down her cheeks. "Oh, Rob, I love him. I can't stand it if he breaks up with me."

28

"Debbie, honey," he murmured, pulling her into his arms. "You can't marry this guy if he's going to beat you."

She yanked away from him. "He didn't beat me. He hit me one time. He was upset."

"Okay, let's start there. What was he upset about at that moment?"

She looked down at the red and gold rug.

Rob waited, but she didn't answer. After several seconds, he sighed in frustration. "I don't know why you're talking to me about this, anyway. I'm not exactly the expert on romance."

She blinked at him. "Is this what it was like for you and Rebecca? I knew she hurt you badly, but—"

"It wasn't all her fault," Rob said, avoiding her gaze.

"Well, it's not all Mark's fault, either."

"Are you sure?"

"Yes." Debbie gulped and looked up at him a little defiantly.

Rob nodded. "Okay. But I can't believe you gave him cause to do this to you."

"I didn't think so. But I can't be perfect for everybody, Rob. Mark expects me to be one way, and Mom and Dad expect something else. I disappointed Mark and he got mad, and just the fact that I'm in this fix has disappointed the folks. Maybe that's it. I'm just—not—perfect."

"Hey, *I'm* not disappointed in you. I just wish I could help you."

He stood holding her and aching for her, not knowing what else to say. But he knew that Mark Elliott had better not come around the Wallaces' house that night.

Chapter 4

At breakfast the next morning, Rob's father ate in silence for several minutes, but he glanced several times at Debbie's disfigured face and scowled. Rob understood his feelings. The puffy bruising around Debbie's eye and cheekbone infuriated him.

"I'm going to call Luke and tell him I'll be in late this morning." Luke was Stewart's assistant manager at his independent hardware store in town.

"What are you going to do?" Connie asked as she took his plate away.

"I'll take Debbie to the police station to file for a restraining order."

Debbie dropped the bagel she'd been holding to her plate. "Dad, if I report this, Mark will have a record. I don't want to mess up his life."

"Like he's not messing up yours?"

Debbie cringed, and Stewart pressed his lips together. Rob knew his father well. He regretted letting his anger surge into the open.

"What if it makes him madder?" Debbie asked. "Have you thought about that?"

"Yes, I have. You need a protective order, Deborah. If Mark changes his ways, fine, but until you know which end is up, you need to get this on record. If you don't report it and something happens later on, the police will want to know why you didn't file a complaint before."

"But—"

"You need to document this. I hope you never need it, but if you do, it will give you some leverage."

"I don't want to make things worse." Debbie rummaged in her pocket and produced a crumpled tissue. "I checked my phone. He hasn't called yet." She blew her nose.

Stewart sighed. "He hasn't called the house phone either." He looked anxiously toward Rob.

Rob took a bite of his Grape Nuts. It would be best if he stayed out of it. Debbie needed his support, but his father would expect him to agree with him. Rob didn't like seeing Debbie and their dad becoming adversaries. They needed to be on the same side right now.

"I hope he's all right," Debbie said shakily.

"*You* hope *he's* all right." Stewart shook his head.

"Dad, he's my fiancé. I love him."

"Funny thing, I don't remember him ever coming around here to see how your parents felt about you marrying him. He's never showed us any respect."

"Daddy!" Debbie's warning was clear.

Rob shifted uneasily as her resistance mounted. Stewart looked hard at him. He wished his father would let it go. Laying down his spoon, he said, "Dad, Debbie knows you want to protect her. Let's not draw lines here."

"I'm not going to stand by and see my daughter abused."

Rob recognized the caged-panther attitude his father had taken. Debbie's injury put him in a lose-lose position. If he criticized Mark, Debbie would resent it. But cutting Mark some slack to appease her might open the door for him to treat her worse in the future.

"Dad," he said.

His father scrubbed a hand across his eyes. "I only want what's was best for you two. I want you to be happy. Both of you. Is that too much to ask?"

Rob was surprised that Dad lumped him in the same category with Debbie. His sister had seemed determinedly happy as she planned her wedding, although her choice of mates had strained her relationship with her parents. Now things had changed where Debbie was concerned. But were the folks upset with him too?

The fact that he hadn't been happy for years must hurt his parents, but he couldn't hide his grief. He supposed his depression was painful for all of them. He'd had a vague notion that dating Brittany would help him move on to a happier place, but so far he was stuck in the same rut.

He poured himself a glass of orange juice and chose the easiest course. He kept quiet. Debbie glared at their father, seemingly on the verge of tears. It was a far cry from the peaceful family breakfast they should be having.

Connie came with the coffeepot and refilled Stewart's mug and Rob's. "Who would you report it to?"

"The county sheriff's department, I guess." Belgrade was too small to have its own police department.

"No," Debbie said decisively. "Until I talk to Mark, I don't think I should do anything." She shoved back her chair and stood.

"Where are you going?" her mother asked.

"Home to Bangor."

"Honey, you need to think about this." Stewart threw down his napkin and rose.

"I've thought about it, Dad. I don't belong here. I should have stayed at the apartment."

Connie wiped her hands on a terrycloth dishtowel, looking from Debbie to Stewart and back.

The wall phone rang, and she went to answer it. Stewart stood facing Debbie determinedly, but Debbie had turned toward the doorway, listening to her mother's end of the phone conversation.

"Hello, Wallaces'."

Rob listened, along with the rest of them.

"Mark?" Connie said.

Debbie took a quick breath and stepped toward her mother, but Stewart reached out and gently held her arm.

33

Connie said, "Yes, she is. Just a minute, please." She turned toward them. "Debbie, Mark's on the phone."

Stewart released her, and Debbie took a shaky step toward her mother.

"Debbie, honey, why don't you let me handle this?" her father asked softly.

"No, Dad. I need to talk to him."

She took the receiver, and Stewart threw up his hands and walked into the living room. Rob and Connie followed. Stewart sat down on the arm of the sofa, and Connie went to stand close beside him.

"We have to step back and let them work through this." Connie surveyed her husband with troubled eyes.

Stewart shook his head in frustration. "I won't have her going back there and getting beaten. If she insists on seeing him again, I want to be there while they talk."

Connie moved in closer and pulled his head against her shoulder. "It's her life, Stewart. We can pray, and we can offer her a safe place, but we can't live her life for her."

He drew a deep breath. "We let Rob live his own life, and look at him now. I don't want to see Debbie end up like he is. Connie, I don't think I can stand to see both of my children miserable."

Connie winced and glanced over her shoulder at Rob.

Standing in the doorway, Rob realized that his father didn't know he had followed them and heard every word. It hurt, but he couldn't do anything about it. His breakup with Rebecca was still a raw wound, and apparently it had hurt his folks worse than he'd known. He looked back at Debbie, who had put the phone to her ear. He couldn't retreat to the kitchen. He crossed the living room quietly and went upstairs to get his briefcase.

When he went back down a couple of minutes later, his mother was sitting on the sofa while his father stared out the front window at the greening lawn and Connie's lush flowerbeds.

Before Rob could say anything, Debbie came in from the kitchen and Stewart turned toward her.

"Well?"

Debbie swallowed hard. Her face was blotchy from crying, and the bruises didn't help things. Rob empathized with his father. He was feeling the protective streak himself.

"He's coming down here tonight, when he gets off work. Can we talk here, or should I meet him someplace else?"

"Here is fine," Stewart said with evident relief.

Connie nodded. "It will give Mark some accountability. Should we expect him for supper?"

Debbie exhaled deeply, as though relieved her father hadn't exploded. "I don't think so. He's working north of Bangor this week. He probably won't get here before seven."

Her mother nodded. "All right, so what's the plan for today?"

"I need to call my boss, and then I'd like to put in a few hours on the computer."

"All right," her father said. "Do you need anything?"

"I think I'm all set, thank you. And thanks for caring so much."

Did Debbie feel the guilt Rob did for putting their parents through this agony? His dad looked so helpless, and that roused Rob's submerged guilt. Dad looked older, more troubled lately. He didn't like thinking he and Debbie had caused that.

"How did Mark sound?" Connie asked in a small voice.

"I don't know. Kind of defensive, I guess."

"Defensive?" Stewart cried.

"That's the impression I got. He was upset that I haven't been answering my phone. He's afraid I mean business."

"Don't you?"

Debbie couldn't meet his gaze. "I love him, Dad. What happened last night was not good, but it doesn't change the fact that I love him and I promised to marry him."

"You can't be serious. You can't stand there and tell me nothing's changed. You have to call this whole thing off, and I mean today."

Debbie bristled at her father's belligerence. "That's not your decision."

Connie stepped forward, her faced creased in worry. "There's time, Stewart. Give Debbie and Mark time to talk and see if they can work things out."

"Work things out? You still think he deserves another chance?"

Debbie raised her chin. "Daddy, I'm an adult. I know you're not happy about any of this, but it's my decision. He wants to talk, and I think I should listen."

Stewart took a deep breath. Rob could almost hear his thoughts, they were so painfully obvious. It wasn't easy for Dad to see his only daughter in this situation. He wanted to jump into the fray for her and right the wrongs Mark had done, but he was denied the privilege. Debbie, on the other hand, couldn't give up on Mark yet, couldn't refuse to hear him out, couldn't stop believing in him.

"I guess I'd better go to work after all," Stewart said.

Relieved, Rob walked toward the side door. "Yeah, I need to get going. See you all later."

Chapter 5

In a rare calm moment at the emergency room, Rebecca grabbed a cup of coffee to sip while she methodically did her paperwork. If no critical patients came through the door in the next thirty minutes, she might get out by five today. It was her turn as charge nurse that day, and she had to stay through the change of shifts and check all the other nurses' charts before she could go home.

Faye came wearily from her station and poured herself a cup of coffee, then sank onto a stool beside her.

"Rough day."

"You said it," Rebecca murmured.

Faye glanced through the glass barrier toward the waiting room. "Quiet now. We're caught up. Can you believe it?" She pushed back a strand of her short red hair.

Rebecca chuckled. "Don't hold your breath."

"Well, my relief just took over. Are you going to be done soon?"

"I have to go over these charts." She grimaced in concentration.

Faye picked up the next one on the stack and glanced down the columns. "They sure used a lot of stuff on that woman who came in with the sprain."

Rebecca frowned as she looked up. "Let me see."

"Was it bad?" Faye asked.

"I didn't think it was *that* bad. Dressings, short splint, cast materials. And we sent her home with pain meds."

"She's being charged for extensive dressing and two sets of meds," Faye pointed out, sipping her coffee.

"Well, they gave her pain killer here and some to take home," Rebecca shrugged. "But what they sent her home with was probably the rest of the six-pack they opened here. Some people charge it that way."

"Doesn't seem right to me. Wouldn't the extra charges bump her up to the next level for payment?"

"Probably." Rebecca picked up another chart and quickly glanced over the procedures and materials that had been used.

"Sometimes it defies logic," she admitted. "Yesterday they charged one of Stacy's patients for three pairs of elastic stockings. *Three* pairs, and the lady was only in here an hour. I asked Stacy about it, and she said they had the wrong size. They opened three packages before they got it right. Now, I ask you, should that woman have to pay for the nurse's mistake?"

"She won't," Faye said flatly. "Her insurance will."

"Right. Which means we all will. No wonder premiums are so high."

Faye looked at her closely then smiled. "Go home and take a bubble bath, Rebecca. Get some rest. This job is getting to you."

"Hey, you're the one who brought it up."

"Two accident victims coming in," their department head, Hilda, called from the triage desk. "Rebecca, could you stay? Lindsay just called in sick. I'll try to get someone to come in for her, but we'll be shorthanded until then."

Faye stood up. "I'm out of here. I hope you didn't have a date tonight."

"Don't worry, my dirty laundry will still be there when I drag myself home."

∞∞∞

Rob was sitting on the wide windowsill in the living room when Mark's dark pickup pulled into the driveway that evening. Debbie had made her mother promise that she and Mark would have privacy for their meeting, but Rob wanted to see him, at least. He wondered if Mark's face would reveal how he could do such an appalling thing to Debbie.

Mark got out of the truck slowly and ambled up the walk, looking the house over as if he'd never been to the Wallaces' home before.

Debbie moved toward the door.

"Don't be so eager, Deborah," her father said dryly.

Connie's troubled look bounced from Stewart to Debbie, and Rob sat silent, feeling powerless.

The doorbell rang. Debbie threw her father a dark look and opened it.

"Hi, Mark."

They stood looking at each other for a moment in the doorway, and Rob tried to see past his sister, for a glimpse of Mark's expression. He stared at Debbie's black eye, and that in itself was mildly comforting. Rob thought Mark seemed a little surprised at the extent of the damage he had done, and wary.

"Hey," Mark said belatedly. "Can we talk?"

Debbie nodded and stepped back into the room.

Stewart and Connie stood. Rob lumbered up from his seat on the windowsill and watched as Mark came in awkwardly and nodded at them, glancing uneasily toward Stewart. Tension crackled in the silence.

"Now, Mark," Stewart began, but Connie stepped forward.

"Debbie and Mark need some privacy," she said firmly. "Let's go out back. I need to show you where I want to plant those bulbs."

Mark looked more hopeful.

"All right," Stewart said grudgingly, "but I expect things to stay civil in here." He followed Connie to the kitchen, looking back over his shoulder.

"I've got some work to do," Rob said, turning to the stairs. He understood his father's feelings of impotence and anxiety, leaving Debbie alone with Mark, but he couldn't very well insist on monitoring the conversation.

"So, what'd you do, skip work today, or what?" Mark growled.

"I brought some work with me. Sit down." Debbie sounded a bit nervous, but neutral.

Rob gained the upper hallway and went quickly to his room and sat down at his desk but left the door open. He wondered how long it would take his sister to fall into Mark's arms, begging him to forgive her for whatever she had done to set him off.

He sat staring at his computer screen, wishing things were different for Debbie. She'd fallen for Mark hard and fast. Their parents weren't crazy about him from the start and had tried to reason with Debbie over the early engagement. They gave up when she seemed to be distancing herself from them, afraid of pushing her into an elopement.

"She's going to marry him anyway," he'd heard his mother say tearfully. "Our attitude now will set the tone for the next several years."

His father had still balked. "He's not good enough for her."

Rob knew it wasn't just a case of the father feeling no man was good enough for his little girl. Mark could be charming, and he was making good money in the construction business, but he had made little effort to win over his future in-laws.

Stewart bridled at Mark's casual attitude toward his elders, and his disrespect when he spoke of his own parents was a red flag. Every time Mark was around, Stewart bristled. His bossiness toward Debbie and her apologetic submission to it had bothered both her father and Rob from the start.

Rob had tried to stay out of it. His miserable track record with relationships kept him from offering an opinion. If Debbie felt Mark was the one, who was he to interfere? Now he wished he'd spent more time getting to know his future brother-in-law, and that he'd drawn Debbie out more about her feelings for Mark.

If he'd gained one thing out of all this, it was caution. He'd kept his relationship with Brittany in the slow lane on purpose, perhaps partly because he saw Debbie rushing toward a destructive marriage. At least Eric had cautioned him, as a friend. Maybe he should have done that for Debbie. He certainly hadn't wanted to see her hurting like this.

But would she listen to him, any more than he listened to Eric? She hadn't listened to her father. Should he, as a brother, have risked alienating her even further by pleading with her to break up with Mark, or at least postpone the wedding?

Downstairs, Mark's heated voice rose, and Rob stood, his adrenaline surging. Debbie's tone was quieter, but edgy. Rob moved softly to the doorway and listened without compunction.

"I said, get your stuff," Mark snarled. "I want you to come back to Bangor."

Rob could barely hear Debbie's reply. "No, I'm not going back if you're still upset."

"I say you are."

"I say I'm not."

Go for it, girl. Rob and Debbie had engaged in hundreds of futile arguments since childhood. Mark would never win.

Mark's angry tones reached him clearly. "Look, I have to be at work in Old Town at 7 a.m. I can't stay here all night arguing. If you want to stay here and pout, all right. Just don't expect me to come all the way down here again and beg. It's not my style."

"I thought we were going to talk about what happened," Debbie said.

"What, that you tossed me out for the umpteenth time when all I wanted was a little show of affection?"

"You know you wanted more than that."

He barked a short laugh. "All I know is, whatever I want, you don't want."

"That's not true." Debbie's voice was coaxing and plaintive. "You know I love you."

"Yeah?" Mark sneered. "It's kind of hard to tell. Think about this, Debbie. If you need marriage, okay. I never refused you that. But this waiting business is too much. You want a wedding ring? I'll get you one. Come with me to city hall within

41

the next week. You got it? Otherwise, it's off. You know how to reach me."

There was a moment's shocked silence. The front door slammed, and Rob stood frozen, unable to believe Mark would walk out like that. The pickup's engine started.

He went down the stairs two at a time. Debbie stood in the living room, staring at the door. She turned toward him, stricken. Rob strode to her, holding out his arms, and Debbie fell against him, sobbing.

"You okay?" Rob asked.

"Y-yes."

"He didn't hurt you again, did he?"

She laughed bitterly. "Not physically."

"I'm sorry, Deb."

Stewart burst through the kitchen doorway. "What happened?"

Debbie took a deep breath and faced her father. "I think I'll be here a day or two longer, Daddy, if you don't mind."

Chapter 6

Rebecca stayed in her apartment the next weekend. The cottage was supposed to be a happy place, where she could get the solitude and rest she needed. Instead, on the one weekend she had gone, she'd cried most of Friday night and half of Saturday. She couldn't keep blubbering over Rob.

So, instead of heading north to Belgrade again, she talked Faye into a Saturday excursion to a large home and garden show at the Civic Center.

"I love this," Faye said dreamily, as they wandered among the exhibits. The scents of earth, verdant foliage, and exotic blooms surrounded them. She stopped before a tiny English garden complete with fountain, bench and garden gate. Live birds chirped in airy cages amid the lush blooms.

"Maine Organic Farming and Gardening Association," Rebecca read off the plaque by the gate. She loved plants, but a potted philodendron and a geranium were the extent of the flora in her apartment. "Imagine having your own house and enough of a yard for a garden like this."

"And enough time to make it look like this."

"You'd have to be rich and hire a gardener, I guess," Rebecca conceded.

Faye laughed. "Well, I don't know about you, but I sure would. I have a purple thumb."

"I used to help my mom with her flower beds. That's before they moved to New Hampshire." Rebecca sighed. "I ought to run down and see the folks tomorrow. I haven't been home since the last week of March."

"Why didn't you go to your cottage this weekend?"

Rebecca moved slowly on toward the next exhibit. She'd never told Faye the details of how she came to own half a cottage. "Too depressing."

"Depressing?" Faye kept step with her. "What's depressing about a lakeside cottage and no commitments for two whole days?"

Rebecca shrugged. "Memories, I guess."

"Bad ones?"

"No, good ones."

Faye considered that. "So make some new ones. Better ones."

Rebecca smiled ruefully. She doubted she would ever have better memories than those of her time with Rob. "Come on, they have a cute little vegetarian café set up over there, and I'm starved. Lunch is on me."

☙❧

Rob felt guilty taking Brittany out. He'd insisted on staying home Friday night to have dinner with Debbie and his parents. But Eric and Leah had invited him over for the first barbecue of the season on Saturday, and his family had urged him to get out.

"Go, have fun," Debbie said, slugging his shoulder. "It's not like we're in mourning."

"Aren't we?" Rob couldn't help recalling his despair when Rebecca had broken off their engagement. Debbie's face fell, and he said quickly, "Sorry. Come with me."

"Forget it. Mom says you've got a very attractive new girlfriend. She'd probably be livid if you took your sister out instead of her."

"Maybe," Rob said, but he'd rather be with Debbie than Brittany.

"Go on, you can't ignore all your friends just because I'm home."

"Are you okay?"

"Of course. Don't I look okay?"

Rob looked her over with mock severity. "Well, other than the yellow and lavender eye, you don't look so bad."

He called Brittany, partly so he wouldn't have to explain to Debbie why he didn't. She was cool to the suggested outing at first, but after an icy minute or two, she thawed enough to accept his invitation to go with him. Rob drove to her apartment with mixed feelings. Trying to avoid his family's pity was a lousy reason to take a woman out.

Brittany kept up a stream of chatter on the way to the Plourdes' house. The historic Lakewood Theater in Madison was producing a full schedule that summer, and she was eager to see some of the shows.

"Should we get season tickets?" she asked, slipping her hand through the crook of Rob's arm as he drove.

"Oh, I don't think so. I'll be gone most of June, but maybe we could take in a show in July."

"Well, I'm getting season tickets," she said firmly. "If you can't escort me to all the plays, I'll ask someone else."

"Fine." Rob could tell she was vexed because the proposal didn't bother him. "Maybe Kayla would go with you."

"Who?"

"You know, Kayla at the office. You go shopping together all the time."

Brittany scowled at him. "As if I'd go to the theater with another woman."

"What's wrong with that?"

"Oh, come on, Rob. Would you go see a show with a guy?"

"Well, yeah, maybe. If it was something I really wanted to see." He threw her a contrite smile. "That's assuming you weren't available, of course."

She smiled then and squeezed his biceps a little. "Of course."

Leah met them at the door and quickly covered her surprise at seeing Brittany.

"Rob! We're so glad you both could make it."

"Thanks for the invitation, Leah." He bent to kiss her cheek and murmured, "I hope you don't mind ..."

She smiled at him, then turned to his guest. "Brittany, isn't it?"

"Yes," Rob said quickly. "You've met, right?"

"I think so," Brittany said. She was sizing up the homey living room that Leah had decorated in bright country prints. "Charming home, Leah."

She didn't sound completely sincere, and Leah colored slightly. "We've been comfortable here, but we're thinking of getting a bigger place soon."

"Surely you can afford it. Eric's been putting in lots of overtime at the office." Brittany started to step toward the sofa, then looked back apologetically. "Or maybe you don't work? I know it puts a cramp in the lifestyle if you have a one-income family."

Rob said, "Leah works at the elementary school part time."

"Just until mid-June," Leah said.

"Oh, you're leaving your job?" Brittany asked.

"Well, I—yes, actually." Leah looked at Rob, then laughed. "Eric was going to make a big announcement later, but ... well, we're expecting."

"Hey, that's great," Rob said, genuinely pleased. "You guys have waited a long time for this."

Leah nodded. "We decided it's time."

"Better you than me," Brittany said, filching a strawberry from the fruit platter Leah had arranged on the counter.

"Well, sure, for now," Leah said, "but you want children someday, don't you?"

Brittany winced. "Please." She turned toward the platter again and maneuvered a sliver of cantaloupe out from among the other pieces of fruit.

While Brittany wasn't looking, Leah looked at Rob aghast, but he just smiled weakly, at a loss for words. The subject of children had never come up with Brittany, and even now that it had, he couldn't picture her in a maternal mode.

Eric came in just then, through the sliding patio door that led to the back yard. "Hi, Brittany. Hey, Rob! Going to help me grill the steaks?"

"Sure, if that's the plan."

"It's too cold out there," Leah protested.

"It hit seventy-five today."

"That was while the sun was up."

Brittany laughed. "You macho men can go cook the steaks. We'll stay in here where it's warm and talk about you."

Rob followed Eric outside, carrying an empty platter for him and feeling a little sorry for unpretentious Leah.

"I thought Brittany wasn't coming," Eric said as soon as the door was closed.

"Sorry. I wanted to bring Debbie, but my family thinks I need a social life."

"No problem. I'm just glad Leah got plenty of steak."

"So, you're going to be a papa."

"What? She told you?"

"Yeah, Leah spilled the beans a minute ago. Congratulations."

Eric grinned. "I wasn't sure now was the best time, but— well, hey, Leah's really happy, and I think it's going to be good for us. We always said we wanted kids."

Rob nodded. "I'm very happy for you."

"You're not just saying that?"

"No, it's terrific." Rob extended his hand, and his friend shook it, still smiling.

"You want kids?" Eric asked, laying the steaks on the grill.

"Well, sure. Some day."

Eric nodded toward the kitchen. "Are you two making progress or not? I figured last week you were having second thoughts about that woman."

"I don't know." Rob sighed. "I like Brit. She just gets a little intense at times, you know?"

"Possessive," Eric said.

Rob frowned. The concept had niggled at him, but he hadn't wanted to say it aloud. "Think so?"

"Know so. She's marked her territory around you. Can't you see how catty she gets whenever another woman looks at you?"

Rob stared at him in surprise. "Other women don't look at me."

Eric laughed. "They would if Brittany wasn't clinging to your arm. Admit it, the thought of you dating someone else panics her. You said she got all green-eyed when you mentioned the cottage."

Rob grimaced. "I didn't tell her it has anything to do with a woman. I think she was just miffed because it's something I want to keep private."

"See? She wants to know every little thing about you."

Rob went to the picnic table and sat down on the bench. "Is that wrong?"

"Does it feel wrong?"

"She wanted to go see the cottage, but I wouldn't take her." Rob paused, expecting Eric to make a snide comment. "I never take anyone there, not even my folks. It's my private spot, you know?"

"Sure. Even I'm jealous. Brittany must be furious."

"She'd love to throw a party there next month, but I nixed that idea."

"Why don't you just tell her about the circumstances of how you came to buy it?"

"Because then she'll ask me a million other questions, and I don't want to talk about it."

Eric shook his head. "Well, buddy, you're going to have to have it out with her sooner or later." He turned to the grill and stabbed one of the steaks with a long-handled fork. "She wants all the details, and you want some space. Sounds rocky to me. Throw me my sweatshirt, will you? It's too early to barbecue."

Rob handed him his gray Bar Harbor sweatshirt and looked over his shoulder toward the patio door. "I guess Leah was right about it being too cold, huh? She's setting the table inside."

48

"Yes, and I'm man enough to admit it." Eric frowned over the steaks. "Hey, just because you were engaged once is no reason for Brittany to go ballistic on you. She should be glad you saw the light and broke up with—what's her name?"

"Rebecca." A twinge of guilt struck Rob as he divulged her name.

"You were young, you made a mistake," Eric said, swinging the fork expressively. "What's the big deal?"

"I don't know." Rob felt traitorous, letting Eric refer to Rebecca as a mistake.

"Maybe the fact that you bought a house together—"

"It's a cottage, not a house. A very small cottage."

"So, why don't you just sell it?"

"I don't want to. I like the cottage."

"So buy Rebecca out. Then it's all yours, and Brittany won't be mad."

Rob kicked at a dandelion bud. "We've been alternating the monthly payments for three years. She pays two thirds of the taxes, and I take care of the maintenance."

"A very tidy arrangement," Eric agreed. "Except things are changing in your personal life, and it's becoming a nuisance."

"No, not a nuisance. I love the cottage."

"Aha! A second ago you liked it. Now you love it."

Rob sighed. "I do. I love it."

"You like Brittany, don't you?"

"Well, sure."

"Really? Because I'm getting mixed signals here. I told you to bring her tonight, and you said no, but at the last minute you changed your mind and brought her."

"I like her," Rob insisted.

"Trust me, Brit won't let you keep her away from the cottage when you're married. Better ask Rebecca now if she'll let you buy her out."

"Hey, just for the record, Brittany and I are *not* talking marriage."

"Okay, buddy, but I'm just sayin'. Buy her out."

"Think so?"

"What are you, nuts? If she won't let you, then sell your half. You can buy another lot on another pond and build a snug little place just the way you want it. Design something modern but cozy."

"I like traditional."

"Okay, traditional and cozy. Lose the baggage, idiot." Eric lifted the steaks onto the waiting platter, and they hurried inside.

Chapter 7

Rebecca had triage duty on Monday. Things were less hectic than they had been the week before. She'd visited her family in New Hampshire on Sunday, spending a quiet day with her parents and sister. Now she felt calmer, more settled, but still melancholy. At noon, she and Faye took their bag lunches to a bench at the edge of the hospital's wide lawn to catch a few minutes of sunshine.

"Got plans this weekend?" Faye asked, unwrapping her sandwich.

"I don't know yet. I was thinking of going to the cottage. It's my last weekend for the month. I can't use it again until July."

Faye shrugged, her eyes twinkling. "Well, I was just thinking maybe we could do something. Maybe a—do I dare to say it? A double date."

Rebecca's jaw dropped. "You've been holding out on me!"

"No, honest I haven't, but ... I met this guy yesterday."

"Where? Not at the hospital."

"No," Faye agreed. "Don't laugh. He's a waiter at that restaurant on Stevens Avenue."

Rebecca frowned. "I don't think I've been there."

"Well, neither had I, but I decided to try something different, and it paid big dividends. He asked me out, and I hedged a little, but I told him he could call me. And guess what? He did!"

"Wow."

"Yeah. But I'm kind of nervous about it, and I thought maybe if I brought my best friend and he dragged along a friend, we could have some fun and I wouldn't be shaking in my boots."

"I don't think so," Rebecca said with a wry face. "I hate blind dates."

"Oh, come on," Faye coaxed. "He's really cute. Rebecca, do you know how long it's been since I had an honest-to-goodness date?"

"If you want to go out with him, go. Just be careful."

"You're not coming, are you?"

She shook her head. "Thanks just the same."

Faye frowned. "You told me once you really cared about someone, but I haven't seen any evidence of a man in your life, and you're far too gloomy to be in love."

"It's a long story."

Faye watched her for a moment without speaking.

"I'll tell you sometime," Rebecca promised.

When she went back to the triage desk to resume her duties, the department head was frowning over a pink charge slip.

"Rebecca, may I see you for a moment?" Hilda asked, glancing up.

"Sure."

"You had a patient with broken ribs who received two IV's?"

Rebecca thought quickly. "One here. The first one was hung in the ambulance."

"Then we'll only charge for one."

"I—that's what I did," Rebecca faltered.

Hilda shook her head. "It says two on this slip."

Rebecca reached for the paper and scanned it quickly. "I'm sorry. I was sure I put down one." She looked closely at the notation, but she couldn't tell if the numbers had been changed.

"Well, it puts the charge up to the next level."

"I understand."

Hilda nodded sternly and turned away. Rebecca swallowed and reached for the stack of charts that had accumulated during her lunch period. It was inexplicable. It was definitely the form she had filled out, but she was certain one dose had been added.

Lord, this doesn't make sense to me, she prayed silently, *but You know everything, so I'll just leave it up to You.* A new serenity stayed with her through the busy afternoon.

Rob pulled into the driveway that evening and stared in surprise at Debbie's car. His sister had left early that morning, declaring she was ready to go back to the office and her apartment in Bangor.

He got out of his car and carried his briefcase to the kitchen door, pulling at his necktie as he walked.

Debbie stood at the counter, peeling potatoes.

"Hey, brother-mine." She grinned at him. "Guess who's back."

"Couldn't cut the apron strings?" He dropped a kiss on the top of her head and gave her a squeeze. "Where's Mom?"

"I'm not sure. Isn't this her day to shop?"

"I guess so. She must be running late."

He put down the briefcase. Debbie resumed her chore, paring the potatoes in long, thin strips that fell into a strainer in the sink. Rob watched her, not sure whether to speak or not.

"Go ahead and say it," she said without looking at him.

"Say what?"

"Oh, whatever comes to mind. *I told you so,* maybe."

"I didn't tell you so."

"Oh, right." She shrugged. "That would be Dad's line. Sorry."

Rob reached out and took hold of her wrist, stilling her hands. "Take it easy with that knife, squirt. Just tell me what happened."

She looked up at him, blinking rapidly, her mouth twisted in pain. "Every time I talk to you lately, I cry."

"It's okay."

She sighed. "I went to the office, and I thought everything was fine. At lunch time I thought I'd go to the post office and pick up my mail." She paused and began stabbing at a potato with the paring knife.

"Easy, kiddo, that poor spud is utterly defenseless."

She glanced up, then threw the knife on the counter. "Rob, he was waiting for me in the parking lot." She buried her face in her hands.

"Who? Mark?" Instinctively, Rob put his arms around her. "Oh, man. I thought he was working in Old Town."

"They finished that job, and he's in Bangor this week. He said he wanted to see me, so he came by to check if my car was at the office and waited for me to come out."

"Okay," Rob said. "Obviously there's more to it than that."

She sobbed and clenched a fistful of his shirtfront. "He wanted me to go with him for lunch, but I told him I had things I needed to do. And he said—" She sniffed and looked up at him imploringly. "He grabbed my wrist, and just then another guy drove into the parking lot and parked right beside me. Mark let go of me, but he said I'd better wait for him after work, or else."

"Or else what?" Rob asked slowly.

"That's all, but it was the way he said it." Debbie turned away in anguish. "You think I'm nuts, don't you?"

"Of course not. Deb, are you scared of him?"

She took a ragged breath, her shoulders heaving. "Yes." She whipped around and flung herself at him. "Oh, Rob, how did I get into this? His eyes were so cold when I said I wouldn't have lunch with him. And he's really strong. You know, he lifts weights."

"Yeah, I figured."

"I was afraid to go to my apartment alone, and—oh, Rob, I can't tell Dad. He'll be so mad. He'll want to call the police, I know, but Mark didn't really *do* anything."

"He threatened you. That's not nothing."

She sighed. "Do you think they'll let me stay here?"

"Of course, but your job—"

"I'm thinking of quitting."

He stared down at her. "Just like that?"

"I don't know. I need time to think. I left an hour early so I wouldn't see him, but I didn't dare go home, so I came right here. But I can't work from home all the time. I asked my boss, and he wasn't very positive. We're coming up on vacation season, and he says they really need me in the office."

"But if you quit ..."

"I know. It's kind of a specialized job, and I probably wouldn't be able to find anything as good down here, but I can't commute this far, and I don't want to live alone up there."

Rob said hesitantly, "Look, I don't want to pry, but when Mark was here last week, he seemed to be pushing you to get married right away."

She nodded, wiping her cheeks with the back of her hand. "He did say that."

"But that's not what you want."

"I don't know what I want right now. But I don't want to feel pressured into something I'll regret later."

"Of course not."

"You think I should just tell him it's over, don't you?"

Rob slipped off his jacket and laid it on the back of one of the pine chairs. "Honestly, Deb, I don't know. If he makes you uncomfortable, then it's probably a good idea to put things on hold."

"But he doesn't want that." She looked down at her hands, then picked up the knife and began peeling another potato. "That's kind of what started this, I think. I wanted to wait, and he didn't."

"You wanted to postpone the wedding?"

"No." She sniffed and gave the potato all her attention.

He watched her carefully for a few seconds as his mind whirled and clicked like a primitive computer searching for data.

"It's the physical thing you're fighting about, then?"

She gave a half shrug. "I don't think he really cares about the wedding. I mean, he'd be perfectly happy if I'd just move in with him."

Rob sighed, leaning on the counter. "Don't rush it, Deb."

"That's what I'm trying to do—not rush it."

Rob scowled. "I thought Mark was a Christian."

"I thought so, too. Maybe he is, or maybe I was kidding myself. I don't know. He seemed to say all the right things at first, but lately ... lately I've had to wonder. He doesn't seem to have the same standards. That's been hard for me. I mean, if he really loves me as much as he says he does ..."

Her bleak expression caught at Rob's heartstrings. "If he loves you, he'll wait the three months, or however long you say." There was no question in his mind about that. Although he'd asked Rebecca to wait repeatedly, and look how that went. He let out a sigh.

"He thinks I'm unreasonable. Maybe I am. Do you think so? I picked August twenty-fourth because we could both get vacation then. Is that a stupid reason to choose your wedding date?"

"Not really. But no matter why you chose it, that's no excuse for him to punch you." It came out fiercely, and Debbie turned to face him, holding the knife loosely in her hand.

"I've upset everybody," she wailed with a sweeping gesture of futility.

"Easy with the knife, sis." Rob took it gently from her hand. "I think you've got enough potatoes there."

"Rob, is it my fault?"

"Absolutely not." He hugged her again, staring over her shoulder into space and time. "Tell me something, Deb. Is it *my* fault?"

"How could it be your fault?" She chuckled weakly. "That's stupid."

"No, I mean ... Rebecca."

"Oh."

"Is it?"

56

Debbie pulled away from him. "You're still bleeding from that, aren't you?"

"I think she hit an artery. I asked her to wait an extra year when I had the chance to go to South America, but it was too much for her."

"I'm so sorry." She hesitated. "What about Brittany?"

Rob pulled in a deep breath. "I don't know."

"Then take my example to heart and end it now, before things get any more complicated."

"All I know is, if it's not right with Mark, don't move things forward. Sometimes you're at the edge of a cliff, and the only safe step you can take is backward."

"You're wondering if that's what Becca did with you?"

"I hope it's not."

"She's still single, isn't she?"

He nodded.

"Is she seeing anyone?"

"How should I know? We don't talk."

"Ever?"

"Not really."

Tires crunched on the gravel driveway, and Rob glanced out the window. "There's Mom. I'd better help her with the groceries. After supper you can help me take my new canoe to the cottage."

"Really? You bought a canoe?"

"Yeah. I thought I could store it in the woodshed there, and maybe Becca can use it. We can take it out tonight." He headed for the door. "I'll break the news to Dad that you're back, if you want. He won't be upset with you. It's Mark that's pushing his buttons."

"Rob."

"What?" He turned back.

"I just wanted to tell you, I'm really sorry about—you know. I thought you and Becca were perfect for each other."

He swallowed hard. "Thanks."

Chapter 8

As the final weekend of the month approached, Rebecca still vacillated on going to the cottage again, wavering when she remembered the feelings of abandonment that had overwhelmed her there.

The memories ought to be less painful as time passed, but they seemed more intense every time she went to Belgrade and knew Rob was only a few miles away. Seeing his personal belongings and knowing he'd been in the cottage recently made every sorrow fresh.

On Friday morning, she packed her bag before going to work but was still ambivalent. She threw in two swimsuits, shorts, jeans, a sweatshirt, extra socks and underwear, and the pioneer's journal she was reading. Then she scrawled a postcard to her parents, just in case they needed to reach her. *Gone to the cottage.* She would mail it at noon if she decided to go.

"So, are you going to your cottage this weekend?" Faye asked when she entered the ER.

"I don't know," Rebecca said. "It gets lonesome up there."

"I thought that's what you wanted—isolation."

Rebecca made a face at her. "There's such a thing as too much solitude."

Faye's pale eyebrows quirked. "I never thought I'd hear you say that."

Rebecca laughed. "Tonight's the big date?"

Faye shook her head sadly. "Nope. We put it off 'til next week. Peter's uncle died, and he had to go home unexpectedly."

"Where's home?"

"Connecticut." Faye smiled ruefully. "I'm pretty sure he's telling me the truth. I mean, a guy wouldn't lie about something like that to get out of a date, would he?"

"With you? Of course not!"

"Well, I didn't think he would, he seems so nice, but I'm not the most confident person in the world."

"Come with me," Rebecca said on impulse.

"To the cottage? You're kidding. That's your private retreat."

"No, really. I want you to go. It would be fun. Swimming and sun. It's supposed to be nice this weekend."

"You're tempting me," Faye admitted.

"Please come," Rebecca said quickly, before she could change her own mind. She hadn't taken anyone to the cottage since she and Rob broke up, not even her sister. "I need company right now. I need you. My bestest friend."

Faye smiled. "What time are you leaving?"

"I'm all packed. I'll do a little shopping after work, while you go home and change. What'll we have? Hamburgers and s'mores?"

"Definitely s'mores," Faye laughed. "Are you sure?"

"Positive. Don't forget your swimsuit."

❧❧❧

Rob packed his briefcase on Friday night and left the office. He half hoped he'd get away without seeing Brittany, but she hovered in the lobby, waiting.

"Hey, are we going out tonight?"

"Well, I dunno." It bothered him that she assumed they had a standing date on Fridays now, without his having to ask her.

"It's a holiday weekend." She fell into step with him.

"Yeah?"

"Yeah. We can do something Monday if you want." Her eyes were bright.

60

"Maybe. I'll check with my folks. They usually want to go to the cemetery and see the parade on Memorial Day."

"The cemetery? That's pretty lame."

Rob turned to face her in the parking lot, swinging his briefcase a little. "Look, Brittany, family is very important to me, and I like to do this."

"What, decorate graves or something?"

He winced. "Yes." He wished she were the type of girl he could talk to about serious, important things. "Besides, my sister's home now. I think I'll be doing family things this weekend."

"We could get together Sunday," she ventured.

"I don't think so." He got in his car and started the engine. The look on Brittany's face as he backed out was not pleasant.

He would have to call her later and apologize. Too bad he was too nice a person to just leave it there and let her steam.

His hands tightened on the steering wheel. Brittany was witty and fun, but sometimes the contrast between her and Rebecca hit him in the face. The comparison made Brittany look like a spoiled brat.

Even the thought made him cringe. He tried not to think about Rebecca. She was sweet, she was kind, she was smart. She would understand about the cemetery. After all, she had been there when Tommy died.

As he drove on toward home, the emptiness that had engulfed him when his younger brother died returned. Every year when Memorial Day drew close, he thought about it. The family would visit the cemetery together. The anniversary of Tommy's death would come a week later.

Tommy had been only twelve years old, a year older than Debbie, when he'd drowned in the lake at their usual swimming place. Rob was fifteen at the time, and the tragedy had hit him hard. It had rocked the whole family and was still a poignant reminder to them all of the brevity of life.

They lived within walking distance of the lake, and their parents had allowed them to go swimming without adults, but never alone. They were all good swimmers from early childhood. Tommy had gone with his friend Jack that day, another twelve-year-old. They had swum out too far, to the little island a quarter mile offshore, a stunt that was forbidden unless someone older was along. Why Tommy had disobeyed, they never knew for sure. Maybe his friend had coaxed him into it. If so, Jack had never admitted it.

Rob felt the tension and sorrow mounting inside him as he drove the ten miles home. Maybe it had been Tommy's idea. He'd been an active, impulsive kid. But it was so senseless. Jack had run home from the lake shaking and crying, and his mother had called the Wallaces. Tommy had disappeared beneath the surface halfway back to shore. Jack claimed he'd dived several times, but it was too deep, and he wasn't sure exactly where Tommy went down.

The state police and a half dozen game wardens had come. Divers had searched between the island and the landing for hours, and at last, in desperation, they'd dragged the bottom with grappling hooks while the devastated Wallaces, Jack's family, and a gathering crowd watched from the shore.

And Rebecca had come and stood with him.

"You shouldn't watch," she whispered, as the boat went slowly back and forth on the gray water.

"I have to."

She stayed with him, turning away with a greenish cast to her face when they brought the body up. Rob left her standing there and ran to the boat landing with his parents. Debbie had screamed, he remembered, and her mother had always regretted letting her be there that day.

Rebecca, he had learned much later, had been sick and hadn't slept well for weeks. Debbie, too, suffered from nightmares. Even in their deepest grief, his parents had not ignored their other two children. If anything, they had begun spending more time with Rob and Debbie, making sure they had pleasant memories of family times together, and supervising them more closely.

It was Rebecca's empathy in his sorrow after the accident that had really drawn Rob to her. She had seen his excruciating grief in its depth. She had gotten on the school bus each day, those last couple of weeks of the school year, and sat down silently beside him in the empty seat the other kids avoided.

When school let out for the summer, she rode over on her bike several times. "I just wanted to see how you and Debbie are doing," she explained to him.

A couple of months later, when he stopped being numb and started feeling things again, he knew he wanted to spend more time with her.

They became close friends, and when she turned fifteen, she'd been his first date, his first girlfriend. His childhood sweetheart, his mother had said fondly. They'd dated his last two years of high school, and he'd never doubted his love for her. They considered going to college together, but Rebecca wanted to go to nursing school, and Rob had a hefty scholarship at a private university in upstate New York.

They'd cried a little over the separation, but the email and phone calls flew thick between Maine and New York for four years, and during the summer after his junior year, he bought her a conservative diamond. When Rebecca finished her nurse's training, she began planning the wedding.

Then Rob had decided he needed to go to grad school. The job—no, the career—he really wanted depended on it. Rebecca's disappointment aggravated him, but he saw the extra degree as necessary. After thrashing it out, he'd thought she understood and could wait for him. Their love was bulletproof—he would have staked his life on it.

But that first year of grad school, with him in California, had put a massive strain on the engagement. Immersed in his grueling studies, he let the communications lapse. Rebecca didn't have a cell phone in those days, but she was lonely and emailed him every day.

He barely had time to read all her messages, let alone answer them. More often than not, he sent a brief note, "I'm fine but busy," or just, "Status quo." He made it home for an unsatisfactory week at Christmas, then he went back to the grind while she lived at home with her folks and worked at the medical center in Waterville.

Another year and they would be together, he'd pleaded that summer. She seemed content with that. They would be married the following June and would find a way for her to accompany him for the last year of school. He thought things were settled. They'd found the cottage before he left for California again. It seemed like everything was perfect when they signed the papers on it. It was the promise of their future together.

He didn't get home that Christmas after all, and the next thing he knew, his future with the woman he loved had blown up in his face.

As he turned in at his parents' driveway, he shoved it all aside. It didn't do any good to try to analyze it. He'd done that for three years, and he hadn't yet been able to discover what had gone wrong. There were a few things he wished he'd done differently—calling her more often, and getting home for Christmas one way or another, but there had to be something more. Anyway, it was too late now.

"Brittany's on the phone," his mother said, as he walked through the door.

"I'll talk to her later."

"Robert! I just told her you were here." Connie had raised her son to be polite, and her disapproval showed on her face as she stood there with one hand over the receiver.

Rob sighed and detoured to take the phone. Why had she called the house instead of his cell phone? Probably because she knew he didn't want to talk to her, but this way he had to.

"Hi, Brittany."

"Honey, what's wrong?"

He looked up at the ceiling. At least when he moved to the cottage next Friday, there would be no land line, and he could turn off the cell phone. He was glad he hadn't told her where the cottage was. He'd have to instruct his mother and Debbie not to give out that information.

"Nothing's wrong. I'm just tired, and I need a break."

"A break from me?" she quavered.

"Well, maybe." He ran his hand through his hair, at a loss for words to explain his feelings.

"I thought things were going good between us." She sounded like she was on the verge of tears, and he didn't want to deal with that. He wished suddenly that May was over and he could retreat to the lake today.

"Look, I'm sorry," he heard himself say, and hated that he had said it. He wasn't really sorry, but he felt pressured to say it, to feel it. "I just think ... things are moving kind of fast here, Brit. I need to have some time to myself."

"You—you mean—" He heard her sniff and winced. "Can we talk about this?"

He sighed. "Okay, but not tonight. Please."

"Call me when you're ready to talk?"

"I will." It was a promise, and they both knew he kept promises. It seemed to mollify her temporarily.

His mother came from the laundry room with a pile of his clean laundry. "Everything all right?"

"Oh, yeah," Rob muttered, taking the stack of T-shirts and socks.

"Brittany seems like a nice girl." His mother's tone was neutral, but her eyes were anxious.

"She's okay." He sighed. "I'm just not sure she's the one, you understand, Mom?"

"Oh, yes, I understand."

He thought he caught a subtle gleam in her eyes. "Well, I don't think Brittany does."

"She's more serious than you are?"

"Way more, and it's funny, but sometimes I feel like I'm just too much of a gentleman to tell her."

"She does seem a little possessive," his mom said tentatively.

Rob snorted. "Yeah, well, I'm glad it's almost June. And, Mom, if she calls and asks you how to find me, please don't tell her where the cottage is."

"All right, Rob."

He eyed her uneasily. "What?"

"I don't see why you're dating her if you don't like her."

There it was again.

"I *do* like her, but I'm not in love with her. At least I don't think so, and I want to take things slow. But she seems to think she owns me now."

"She can't think that if you don't let her."

"Okay, okay. I get the message."

She put her hand on his arm. "Take your time, Rob. You're young."

"Mom, I'm twenty-seven."

"I know, but ... this thing with Debbie and Mark is really scaring me."

"I think she's coming around, Mom. She just needed time to sort out her loyalty and her common sense."

"She's still wearing the diamond."

"Things may change soon."

Connie exhaled sharply. "She stayed at work all day today. I hope he's left her alone. She wanted to go to her apartment and get some things tonight."

"Is she going to let the lease run out?" Rob asked.

"I don't think she's made that decision yet. We're praying so hard."

Rob felt a pang of guilt. He hadn't been praying, though he worried about his sister constantly. He knew his parents were praying for him, as hard as they were for Debbie. He was sure they had never stopped. He wished he hadn't, and that he could take his own problems and Debbie's before the Lord and know his petition would be heard. But he'd ignored God too long for that.

"What's the plan for Monday?" he asked, partly to change the subject and partly to cement the alibi he had given Brittany.

"Well, the usual, I guess. Cemetery, parade, picnic lunch. I've got plants for Grandpa and Grandma Wallace's graves, and Tommy's." Her voice broke a little on his brother's name. "Is that all right with you?"

"It's fine. I'm glad we'll all be together." On impulse, he stooped and kissed her cheek. "Hey, what's this? A gray hair? Did I do that?" Grinning, he touched the crown of her head, where several silvery strands were showing.

She smiled sweetly. "You and your sister." She hesitated. "If you want to invite Brittany ..."

"I don't think it's her idea of a good time, but thanks for offering." He picked up his briefcase and headed upstairs with it and his clean laundry. As he changed into casual clothes, he tried to picture Brittany fitting into the Wallace family's routine.

Brittany and Debbie, setting the table for the picnic. Brittany and his mother, canning mincemeat together, or stitching a quilt. Rebecca had done those things with his mother that last summer, before things fell apart. He had a photograph on his computer of them shelling peas together. He couldn't get rid of it; it was too painfully precious.

He'd never had the chance to display pictures of Rebecca on his desk at work, the way Eric did of Leah, but sometimes he looked at the old photos.

Her senior picture always made him smile, with her eager air of joy and anticipation. Her father had snapped the one that made him cry. In it, he and Rebecca were sitting on the porch swing at the Hardings' old house, before her family moved out of state. He sat with his arm confidently around Rebecca with a lopsided, contented grin, and she, in the denim overalls that made her look like a kid, sat comfortably beside him, smiling, not at the camera, but at him.

He was thankful that Brittany hadn't offered him any pictures of herself. Had he ever imagined she could mean as much to him as Rebecca had?

He'd called Rebecca's father in bewilderment from California, after she sent him the fateful letter in March three years ago. Her father had been Dad Harding back then.

"I just don't understand," Rob had told him. "Is she serious? I love her."

67

"Yes, son, I'm afraid she's serious. She can't take any more of this three-thousand-miles-apart business. And now it seems you're not coming home in May, but you're jetting off to Buenos Aires instead."

"But it's only until—"

"Rob, you asked her to put things off another year, and she's had enough. This is really wearing on her, and she's throwing in the towel. I'm really sorry."

Rebecca wouldn't talk to him, though he'd begged her father to call her to the phone.

When he squeezed out a week to fly home in late May, she had already gone with her family to their new home in New Hampshire. He'd called several times, pleading to be allowed to drive down and make his case, but she refused to talk to him on the phone or in person. Finally he gave up, driving past her old house several times in confusion. He couldn't help wondering if she'd met someone else. It didn't make sense to him.

She had changed her e-mail when they moved, and she didn't give him the new one. He wrote a stilted note by hand, telling her to please keep the ring, and asking what she wanted to do about the cottage.

With her father's intercession, they had hammered out an agreement for making the payments and alternating use during the warmer months. Neither could afford to buy the other out, and both, it seemed, wanted to keep their interest in the property. His heart in tatters, he'd gone to Brazil.

He'd spoken to her twice since then. Twice, in over three years. When she took the job at the hospital in Portland, he called to check the new address. She was always prompt in her payments, and he sent her a postcard each spring after he'd gotten the cottage ready for her.

The second winter he'd called to tell her the place had been broken into. They didn't keep anything valuable there, and there wasn't much damage, just a broken window. It could have been a lot worse. She'd been concerned, but she'd asked him to take care of it and curtailed the conversation when he asked her how she'd been.

It was clear she didn't want him in her life anymore, other than as half owner of the cottage. He had tried to do what she wanted and left her alone.

Chapter 9

"You didn't tell me you had a canoe," Faye squealed.

"I didn't know." Rebecca squeezed into the shed behind her. They'd gone in search of more firewood and had found a new Old Town canoe sitting on sawhorses inside the shed behind the cottage.

"There's a note." Faye pulled a sheet of paper from beneath one of the paddles.

Rebecca took it to the doorway and squinted at it in the twilight.

Hope you don't mind, I brought this down for storage. Thought you might like to use it. Rob

"Hey, I like this guy!" Faye took a quick inventory. "Two paddles, two life jackets. There's even a fishing rod and a tackle box in here. You want to take it out?"

Rebecca glanced toward the lake. "It's a little choppy tonight. Maybe tomorrow, if the wind dies down."

"All right, let's get the wood."

They cooked their hamburgers on the gas stove in the kitchen, then settled in front of the fireplace.

"Want to play a game?" Rebecca asked.

Faye surveyed the rough bookshelves that lined the end wall of the room. "Wow. You and old Rob must have been serious game players."

Rebecca smiled faintly. "We never stayed here together. We started stocking it for—well, for our honeymoon, I guess, and after. It seems like every year Rob brings something new and leaves it. We started out with Monopoly and Rook, and now we've got all these games."

"Who do you play with?"

Rebecca shrugged, scanning the boxes. Apples to Apples, Trivial Pursuit, Balderdash. "Maybe Rob brings his friends."

"Are those his books too?"

"Some are his, some are mine. A few were actually here when we bought the place." She pulled *Helen's Babies* from the shelf. "Cute old stories. Rob leaves mysteries every summer, and I usually contribute a historical or two."

Faye watched her curiously. "Do you ever read his books?"

Rebecca turned away to hide her discomfiture. "Sometimes." She didn't tell her friend that she always went through the shelves when she came, looking for new arrivals, and took them down to examine them. Once in a while, she found one where he had written his name in the front, and it made her grieve all over again, but she still did it.

"You said he's an architect, right?"

"Yeah. Works for a company in Waterville. It's what he always wanted to do."

"Is he happy?"

"I suppose so. I'm not really sure." Rebecca flipped her long braid back over her shoulder. "Hey, let's take our stuff upstairs and make up the beds."

They carried their overnight bags up the narrow stairway.

"There's a powder room there, and two bedrooms," Rebecca said.

"Which one is yours?"

"I usually use this one, but the other one has bunks. If you want this one—"

"No, that's fine," Faye assured her. "You and Rob keep linens here?"

"Yes. I used to bring them with me, but after the first summer it seemed silly, so I picked up some sheets and towels at yard sales and just left them here. Rob does it, too, I think. There were a couple of new coffee mugs and towels the last time I came."

"And now a canoe," Faye said.

Rebecca shrugged and took the single sheets from the drawer of the rickety pine dresser in the bunk room. "He always liked boats and fishing. Guess he got tired of the leaky old rowboat and decided to buy a canoe."

As they spread the sheets, she wondered if Rob ever brought anyone else here. He must, or why all the board games? She always dusted before she left, even the unused bunk room.

If the Wallaces ever came here, she supposed they would take the double bed, and Rob would sleep in a bunk. Or maybe he had weekend parties here with his friends. Why not? But she doubted that. It wasn't Rob's style. The place was always spotless when she arrived, with no evidence of rowdiness. She felt somehow that Rob used the cottage the way she did, for a place of solitude and peace.

The next morning, the lake was flat and smooth as a mirror.

"Let's take the canoe out," Faye coaxed.

Rebecca gave in, and they were soon paddling toward a half-acre island in the middle of the lake. Rebecca sat in the stern, paddling with strong, sure strokes, coaching her friend through her first canoeing experience.

"What's that?" Faye cried, pointing her dripping paddle off toward the north end of the lake.

Rebecca squinted and focused on a bobbing shape.

"A loon."

"You're kidding."

"Nope." Its quavering laugh came to them across the water.

"Awesome," Faye breathed. "Is that one over there?"

Rebecca turned to focus on the second object of curiosity. "No, that's a snag."

"What's that? Some weird bird?" Faye's orange life jacket clashed mercilessly with her bright hair.

Rebecca laughed. "No, idiot. It's the end of a log sticking out of the water."

"Oh, you mean there's a big old log underwater there?"

"Yup."

"Probably rotten and slimy."

"Exactly."

Faye shuddered. "Remind me not to go swimming over there."

"Ship your paddle," Rebecca ordered. "We're almost there, and I'll bring us in."

The bow slid with a crunch onto the sandy shore of the island.

"Who owns this place?" Faye asked, looking around as Rebecca hauled the canoe part way up onto the beach.

"Last I knew, an old guy in Belgrade Village. His family's owned it forever. I don't think they mind the occasional friendly trespasser."

"Have you ever been out here before?"

Rebecca nodded, slowly surveying the pines and the rocky shore. "I've rowed out a few times, and ... Rob and I rowed out here the day after we signed the papers on the cottage."

"Really?"

"Yeah, we brought a picnic and ..." she let it trail off and led the way over the rocks to the spot where she liked to sit and look at the cottage. She *wouldn't* think about that day.

He had been so happy, and she had been near bursting with love and hope. It had been the perfect day. They'd lingered at the cottage later, exploring their new property and planning for the next summer. Two days later, Rob was on the plane to California.

"Why did you break up, anyway?" Faye asked softly.

Rebecca shrugged. "He—he went away for a long time, and it seemed like he just forgot me. He was in grad school, and he quit calling. I didn't hear from him, and when I did, it was just a few words. He finally called and said he was so busy he didn't have time to write anymore."

"Grad school is tough," Faye offered.

Rebecca grimaced. "How long does it take to send an email? I didn't have a cell-phone then. Couldn't afford it yet. And then he didn't come home for Christmas. Too expensive, he said, and he had a big project he was working on."

74

"So you called it quits."

"Not right away. I mailed him his present."

"What was it?"

"An afghan. I crocheted it myself."

"Did he like it?"

"He didn't say."

"Ouch."

"Yeah, well, I waited a few weeks and sent a rather pouty letter, I'm afraid, asking again why he couldn't take a few minutes to write to his fiancée."

"And?"

"And he didn't write back. His mother called me later and told me he'd been picked for a summer internship in Buenos Aires. Can you believe it? He didn't tell me. I had to hear it from his parents, that he wanted to postpone the wedding another year. I was so ripped."

Faye nodded in sympathy. "Not the most sensitive man alive, I'd say."

Rebecca turned on her fiercely. "That's just it. He was. I don't know why he acted that way that winter. It wasn't at all like him."

"Maybe he was just tired."

Rebecca shook her head. "I was so hurt. I figured there must be another girl. What other logical explanation could there be?"

Faye opened her mouth, but Rebecca jumped back in. "I tried to call him at his dorm, but he wasn't there. His roommate told me he was off at some fabulous leadership conference, but he didn't have a phone number he could give me." She tried to blink back the tears. "At the time I figured maybe his roommate just didn't want to give it to me, or maybe Rob had even told him not to."

"You think he wanted to break up with you?"

Rebecca stooped for a pebble and tossed it into the water. "Not now, I don't, but I wasn't exactly rational then. I tried to get hold of him for three days. I wanted to hear it from him. But it was like he'd fallen off the edge of the planet. Finally, I sat down and wrote him a Dear John letter."

"That didn't bring him to his senses?"

"He called about a week later, but by that time I was convinced he was unforgivable. I needed him, and he wasn't there." She shook her head at her own immaturity. "I made my father talk to him. I wasn't going to let him off easy. I told my dad I didn't ever want to speak to Rob again. And he told Rob. And Rob believed him."

Faye listened, her green eyes troubled. "So, it's your father's fault?"

"No, silly, of course not. It's my own stupid fault." Rebecca dashed away a tear. The loon was swimming closer to the island, and she could see its long, sharp bill and its glossy, mottled feathers. "Come on, let's go back."

�☯�

Rebecca insisted on attending church on Sunday. She knew Faye wasn't in the habit of going to church, and she had approached the subject warily, but her friend agreed as if it were another novel outing, like the garden show. Rebecca gave the location some thought and chose a small church in Augusta, in the opposite direction from the one she'd attended as a child. She didn't want to take a chance of running into Rob's family.

"That was nice," Faye said awkwardly in the car afterward, as Rebecca pulled out of the parking lot.

"I'm going to start going to church again every Sunday," Rebecca said quietly, more to herself than to Faye.

"Even in Portland?"

"Yeah. I'll find a church there." She turned onto Route 11, toward Belgrade.

"Do you believe all that about God hating sin?" Faye asked a little belligerently.

"Yes. If He put up with lying and cheating and anger and all those other things, He wouldn't be God."

Faye frowned. "I thought God was love and peace and joy, all that good stuff."

"Well, He is, but He has to deal with the sin first."

Faye stared out the window for some time. At last she turned to look at Rebecca in confusion. "You're not a sinner."

Rebecca laughed aloud. Her reaction clearly startled her friend. "I'm sorry, Faye. I just can't help it. If you think I'm not a sinner, you either don't know me, or you don't know what sin is."

Faye's shoulders slumped. "Oh, right. What did you ever do? You're honest to a fault, I know that. You haven't robbed any banks that I know of."

"For starters," Rebecca said softly, "I think I'm the most self-centered person I know."

"That's crazy."

"No, it's not. I used to love my job because it allowed me to help people who really needed help. Now ... it's just a job."

"It's a very stressful, tiring job," Faye countered.

"We've been friends all this time, but I've never told you that I think spirituality is important."

"Is it really?"

Rebecca nodded, fighting back tears. "Knowing God is more important than anything else. And if I know that and don't tell the people I care about ... well, it was wrong of me, and I'm sorry."

Faye frowned. "You're a good person."

Rebecca shook her head in protest. "Don't say that. I've hurt a lot of people."

"You mean ... Rob?" Faye watched her cautiously, as though afraid she would explode in rage or grief.

In her mind, Rebecca thought of all the people she had wounded. Her parents, the Wallaces, Rob most of all. Softly she said, "I'm starting to think maybe I hurt him even more than he hurt me. A lot more."

"Not possible."

Faye reached out and gave her arm a squeeze, but Rebecca couldn't hold the tears back any longer. She pulled the car to the shoulder of the road and reached for a tissue. "You drive."

⚜

Rob dug a neat hole in front of Tommy's headstone and stood back so his mother could kneel and place the budding azalea bush in it and tamp the extra earth in around it.

"That looks nice, Mom," Debbie said softly.

Connie started to rise, and Rob reached out to give her a hand. They stood together, looking at the bush and the stone, with the deeply carved letters. *Thomas H. Wallace, beloved son.* Stewart turned away first and walked slowly across the gravel path to where his parents were buried. Rob watched him, wishing he could do something to ease his father's pain, but his own was so strong he didn't see how he could help.

"He was so full of energy." Connie sighed and glanced at Rob. "Not like you. You were a thoughtful boy. Tommy was just ... a bundle of motion."

"I thought he was such a brat," Debbie choked out, and Rob stepped up between them, putting one arm around his sister and one around his mom.

"Maybe it wouldn't hurt so bad if we quit coming here," he said tentatively.

Connie shook her head emphatically. "I don't want it to stop hurting."

Rob eyed her in surprise. "Isn't it supposed to mellow out into fond memories and regret?"

"Regret?" Connie said. "Maybe, for the loss of his future, but ... mostly I'm thankful we had him twelve years. He was so different from you kids."

"We used to call him the alien," Debbie remembered. "Rob and I told him he was adopted because he wasn't like us. Those blue eyes!" Tears streamed down her cheeks.

Connie smiled. "He had your Grandma Wallace's eyes."

78

"He'd get really mad. I think we upset him. Mom, we were mean to him." Debbie swiped at the tears, and Rob squeezed her shoulder.

"No use fretting about it now," Connie said. "That's the way with sisters and brothers. He knew you loved him."

"I hope so." Debbie's voice broke.

Stewart came back slowly, wiping his eyes, and stopped near them. "There's something I want to say."

Rob and Debbie faced him expectantly. Connie stepped to her husband's side and took his hand.

"Robert, Deborah," their father said solemnly, "we don't know how much time we have on this earth as a family. I want to see you kids happy. I've stood back and watched you two beating your heads against a wall. You know what? It hurts as much as losing Tommy, only it takes longer."

Rob stared at him in surprise, and he felt Debbie's tension, too, but Connie gazed at her husband with pride.

Stewart glanced toward the road, where people were lining the parade route.

"Listen, kids, I'm only going to say this once. Well, that's the plan, anyway. If you don't shape up, I may have to say it again." He eyed them both sternly. "Get things right with the Lord. Do it today." He pulled his handkerchief out and blew his nose. "There. I've said my piece. Should have said it a long time ago. Maybe would have saved you both some agony, I don't know."

Connie rubbed his arm, waiting to see if he was done.

Rob cleared his throat, unable to come up with an appropriate response. His father was right. It was high time he faced his spiritual apathy. Faith should not depend on feelings, but he had let his depression strangle his belief for years, and he'd stopped caring whether he measured up to God's standard or not.

He looked at Debbie. Her eyes glistened. Their father's admonition had hit home with her, too.

Stewart swung his arms wide. "All right, let's go watch a parade or something." They all chuckled and headed for the car.

Rob scraped the dirt off the blade of the spade with the edge of his sneaker while his father lifted lawn chairs from the trunk.

Chapter 10

Rebecca and Faye slathered on sunscreen and canoed across the lake Monday morning, where they picnicked on the beach of the music camp. In a few weeks the place would be swarming with youngsters, but not yet. It was peaceful beneath the huge white pines, and they stretched out luxuriantly on the bed of sand and dried pine needles.

"I adore long weekends," Faye murmured sleepily.

"Mm. Think the hospital would consider going to a four-day work week?" Rebecca picked up a perfect pinecone and fingered the sharp points of its scales.

"My folks are probably listening to the Gettysburg Address right about now," Faye said.

"My family used to go, when we lived in Belgrade." Rebecca sighed. "I don't know if they go to the parade in New Hampshire. It's not like they're near the cemetery where our ancestors are buried."

"Why did they move down there?"

"Dad's job. They didn't want to sell the old house, so they're renting it out now. I think they plan to retire back here someday."

"Who lives there now?"

Rebecca shrugged. "Some family with kids. I saw a bike and some other toys on the lawn the last time I drove by. I just hope they don't destroy the place."

Faye rolled over on her side and propped her head up on her elbow. "Do you think I'm a sinner?"

Rebecca closed her eyes for an instant in silent prayer. "Why do you ask?"

"Just wondering. I've been thinking about it since yesterday. You know. Church."

"The Bible says all have sinned."

Faye collapsed on her back as though deflating. "I guess that means I am. I've been comparing myself to you, and if you're a sinner, I guess I must be a real reprobate."

"Is that so?"

Faye made a wry face. "Well, sure. I'm selfish, too, you know. You don't have a corner on that. And proud, I guess. I tried to tell myself I'm not, but I didn't believe me."

Rebecca chuckled.

"And I'm not above telling white lies," Faye admitted.

"Don't despair." Rebecca smiled. "The Bible also tells you what to do about it."

The pale eyebrows shot up. "What do I do?"

"Well, it's not really so much doing, as believing."

Faye was pensive. "Okay. What am I supposed to believe?"

Rebecca rose and dusted off her shorts. "Let's go back to the cottage. It's easier to explain it if I have my Bible handy. It's been a long time since I talked to anyone about this, and I'm a little rusty."

"All right." Faye got up, wincing. "My aching arms! You didn't tell me canoeing was such hard work. I'm going to be sore all week!"

❧❦❧

Rob had scheduled the first week of June as vacation. Throughout his last day of work, he wished he was out on the lake, but he kept diligently at his assignment.

He was packed and ready to retreat to the cottage on Saturday, June first. He would have preferred to go Friday night, but, even though he knew Rebecca wouldn't be there, it was still May thirty-first, and he scrupulously avoided intruding on her time. He had determined long ago that he would never consciously give her a reason to resent his actions.

When he was ready to leave, he stopped by Eric's desk, where his friend was packing up his drawing materials.

"See you a week from Monday," Rob said.

Eric grinned at him. "Relax, bud. Enjoy yourself."

"Thanks." Rob took the stairs, not the elevator, but even so, Brittany caught him in the lobby.

"So, we won't see you at the office for a week." She walked out into the parking lot beside him.

"That's right."

"Will you call me?"

"No phone," he said apologetically.

"You have a cell phone, Rob."

He shrugged. "The reception is poor at the cottage. I like it that way."

"What if someone needs to get in touch with you from work?"

"No, that's not going to happen. I'll be as incommunicado as if I were off to Timbuktu. The bosses know that."

She tried again as he approached his car. "I'd really love to see this place that has such a hold on you, honey."

He smiled and said firmly. "Afraid not. I've decided to keep it private, at least for now."

She turned toward him. "Well, at least drive me home. I'm not going to see you for a whole week and two weekends."

"I need to take care of some last-minute things, so I can get off early in the morning."

Her laugh was brittle. "Sounds like an arctic expedition."

"No, it's not far, but it's an important retreat for me. I can get off alone there and unwind. Do you understand?"

"Not really." She cocked her head to one side. "Pretty please?"

Rob sighed and dredged up a smile. "Okay, hop in." He clicked the remote to unlock the car and opened the passenger door for her.

What am I doing?

He tried to keep the conversation impersonal and light as he drove the short distance to Brittany's apartment building. When he parked outside the entrance, he didn't shut off the engine, but started to open his door. He'd walk her to the front door and then skedaddle.

Brittany reached toward him hungrily. Rob hesitated, reluctant to fuel her ideas of what their relationship was becoming.

"Come here," she whispered.

"Brit, I—"

She stamped her foot. "Be quiet and kiss me. Please?"

He looked down at her lovely face and swallowed. "I don't think I should. In fact, I think we should cool things off."

Her mouth skewed. "Rob, don't do this. Please don't." Her dread was palpable, and his guilt was enormous. He had definitely let the relationship go too far. He had given in to her over and over, thinking he could break it off when the moment was right. But how could he?

He'd been amazingly naïve. He'd hoped he could ease out of the relationship, the way he'd eased into it, gradually weaning her from the dates and luncheons, cutting off the kisses, until they were back to being just friends. Somehow he'd imagined that was possible. He couldn't just brutally cut her loose. That was what Rebecca had done to him, and he knew that he couldn't do it to someone else.

Whether he liked it or not, he would continue to see Brittany frequently at work, and knowing he had caused her pain would haunt him forever. Her vibrant blue eyes swam with tears as she waited woefully for him to make a move, toward her or away from her.

She was going to hate him, no matter what he did. Even his father would despise him if he knew he'd toyed with Brittany's emotions for weeks. He hadn't thought she was that serious at first, and now that he knew he needed to back away from her, he could see that she was very attached to him. She wasn't the ice princess Eric had made her out to be. Her lower lip trembled as she waited, holding her breath.

"I'm sorry, Brit. I'll see you next week." He bent his head and pecked her on the cheek, but she clung to him, with both hands around his neck. She kissed him back, until he turned his head a little and their lips met. His trouble radar began to signal as she pressed against him seductively, and he put his hands up to hers, gently loosening her clasp, then broke off the kiss. "I'll see you a week from Monday."

He pulled back as he said it and fumbled for his door handle. Before he could get out, she was out of the car and striding, almost running toward the building.

Chapter II

That first morning at the cottage, Rob opened the refrigerator to stow his groceries and found a half-full carton of milk and a quart of strawberries. It was too early for Maine strawberries, so he knew Rebecca had bought them at the store. He wondered if she had meant to leave them for him, or if she'd forgotten to take them. Rebecca loved strawberries.

The tackle box was on the floor in the shed, and his rod was leaning against the woodpile. His note was gone. He examined the canoe carefully and decided with satisfaction that she had used it. Both life jackets were in the bottom. He wondered fleetingly if she'd had help launching it and decided not to think about that.

It was a tremendous relief to be away from the office and the phone. He swam several times a day, took the canoe out, and fished for hours. On Tuesday afternoon he lay on the sofa, lazily sipping a Dr. Pepper and reading a detective novel. He laid the book on his chest after a while and let his mind drift.

This was the time to settle things. His dad was right. It was time to get rid of the ambivalence and uncertainty. If he knew he was walking where God wanted him, dealing with Brittany would not be difficult. It was time to let go. That would mean telling her decisively that he didn't want to go out with her anymore.

Simple, right?

His pulse had accelerated just thinking about how she would react.

Deliberately, he turned his attention elsewhere. His gaze roved over the bookshelves above his feet, and fell on an unfamiliar volume. He sat up and stretched to reach it. *The Annals of Fort Bridger*. Next to it was *The U.S. Cavalry, 1840-1878*. He smiled. Rebecca had not lost her penchant for history. Apparently she was going through an American West phase.

Further scrutiny rewarded him with a slim volume, *The Diary of Samuel Boyden, Emigrant*. He flipped through it and found it was the published journal of a man who left Maine to go West in 1845.

He wondered if she was doing research for a book. Rebecca had always wanted to write, and during their courtship he had promised her that he would support the family while she followed her yearning. She didn't need the nursing degree, he'd insisted. She could stay home and have babies and write novels.

So much for that plan. Now she was supporting herself on her nurse's pay, as far as he knew. Her address was for an apartment in Portland. No babies, and he hadn't heard about any novels. Was she happy? He hoped so. No, that wasn't true. He couldn't truly hope she was happy alone.

The next day he poked his head into the spare room and spotted a sheet of paper on the dresser. Curious, he went in and picked it up.

Rob, I don't know you, but I wanted to say thanks for letting us use your canoe and your cottage. I know it's half Rebecca's cottage, but anyway—from everything she tells me, I think you're a pretty nice guy. We had a fabulous, low-key weekend. Another friend of Rebecca's, Faye

She had brought a friend here, a girl friend. Rob smiled and tucked the note into his shirt pocket.

∞

An ambulance brought an elderly woman with chest pain to the ER Tuesday morning. Rebecca stood for nearly an hour in the curtained cubicle, holding the patient's hand. She had set up the heart monitor and blood oxygen clip, and she'd started oxygen and an IV line. The doctor had come in to examine the patient and ordered medications, and now they were waiting for a cardiac nurse to come move the woman upstairs.

"Mrs. Watson, is there anything I can do for you?" Rebecca asked, gently trying to disengage her hand from the old woman's clasp.

"Don't leave me," the patient pleaded.

"I'm not going far," Rebecca promised.

"Stay," Mrs. Watson breathed, and Rebecca heard fear and desperation.

"Your daughter should be here soon." Rebecca stroked the old woman's fingers. She reached up and tenderly pushed back a strand of white hair that had fallen down over the wrinkled brow. "You remind me of my grandma," she confided with a smile.

Mrs. Watson's eyes widened. "You're a good girl."

Rebecca accepted the praise without comment, wishing she could reach the stool in the corner so she could get off her feet for a few minutes. She ought to fill out her paperwork and take another assignment, but she didn't want to leave Mrs. Watson alone when she so clearly needed someone with her. Gradually the old woman relaxed, and her grip on Rebecca's hand loosened.

Another nurse, Stacy, in her soft blue uniform, opened the curtain.

"Right in here. Rebecca, this is Eileen Marcoux, Mrs. Watson's daughter."

"Mama," the middle-aged woman cried, stepping quickly to the side of the gurney and reaching for her mother's hand. Mrs. Watson's eyelids flew up.

Rebecca greeted Mrs. Marcoux soberly. "Hello. I'm Rebecca Harding. I'm your mother's nurse here in the ER. She'll be going upstairs soon to the cardiac care unit."

Mrs. Marcoux nodded. "How are you doing, Mama?" She leaned toward her mother, speaking loudly, then straightened and focused on Rebecca. "Has the doctor been here? How is she? They said she had a heart attack."

Rebecca nodded. "She had a mild myocardial infarction. She seems stable now, but the doctor thinks we ought to keep her overnight and monitor her."

"What are all these wires and tubes for?"

Patiently, Rebecca explained each piece of equipment and tried to reassure both the patient and her daughter.

"Can she hear me?" Eileen asked.

"Oh, yes. We were having a nice conversation when you came in. Isn't that right, Mrs. Watson?"

The elderly woman raised her chin a little. "I hear you, Eileen. I'm not deaf."

"Mama, how do you feel? Are you in pain?"

"Not so much now," Mrs. Watson quavered. "It was bad at first."

"Can I see the doctor?" Eileen turned toward Rebecca again.

"Of course. Why don't you stay with your mother, and I'll go see if Dr. Theron is still in the ER."

When she returned a few minutes later, Eileen was seated in a chair, still holding her mother's hand in silence, but her lips moved. Mrs. Watson's eyes were closed, as she lay weak and vulnerable on the stretcher.

Rebecca hesitated, thinking surely Eileen was in prayer for her mother. After a moment, she opened her eyes and looked at Rebecca expectantly.

"Dr. Theron is with another patient, but he says he'll come in and talk to you in just a few minutes," Rebecca said.

"Thank you. I should call my brothers, but I'd like to speak to the doctor first, so I understand her condition better before I call them. And I'll want to call her pastor too."

"Of course." In the space of a breath, Rebecca sent up a prayer for guidance. "Mrs. Marcoux, do you trust in God?"

The woman's eyes flared, then she smiled. "Yes, I do. I'm very worried about Mama just now, but I know He'll do what's best for her."

Rebecca nodded. "I'll be praying for her," she whispered.

"Would you pray with me now?" Eileen asked.

She couldn't refuse, and Mrs. Marcoux had mentioned the pastor first. She hoped that counted, if any of the other staff heard her praying with the relative of a patient. The practice was generally frowned upon at Ainsley Hospital.

"Of course." Rebecca prayed earnestly but briefly, hoping the doctor would not appear in the middle of things.

When she was finished, Eileen said softly, "Thank You, Lord, for taking care of Mama, and for giving her a nurse who loves You and understands. If it's Your will, please heal Mama and strengthen her. Amen."

"Would you like me to call the pastor for you?" Rebecca asked.

"You can do that?"

"Certainly, if you ask me to. I can't go with you up to the CCU, and it might be nice if you had the pastor here to support you."

"Yes, it would. It's time for Rick and me to think about bringing Mama into our home. She's wanted to be independent, you know, but I think it's time."

Rebecca took the pastor's phone number and went to the desk. Stacy was the charge nurse that day, and the sidelong look she shot her troubled Rebecca.

The CCU nurse came in while she was on the phone, and Rebecca saw her take Mrs. Watson to the elevator with Eileen following. At last Rebecca was able to begin filling out the pink and purple charge slips, carefully reviewing all her notations before she filed the chart for Stacy to check.

Chapter 12

Stewart scanned the shelves in the plumbing section of the hardware store, making notations on the re-ordering form his clipboard held. Everyone was doing repairs this time of year, and business was brisk. Paint, shingles, a thousand things.

A man approached him and stopped at the end of the aisle. Stewart glanced toward him with a cordial smile.

"May I help—Say! Ed Harding! How've you been?"

Ed grinned and extended his hand to Stewart. "We're fine. I'm up here to do a little maintenance on the house, and I figured I'd give you the business."

"I appreciate that. Are the tenants tearing the place down?"

"Oh, nothing serious. Kids are rough on any house. I just need some screws and duct tape and a quart of paint."

Stewart nodded. "Let me know if you can't find what you need."

"I'll do that."

"I don't suppose you and Myra are going to move back up here soon?"

"Not for a few more years, but we'd like to come back here eventually. We miss all the neighbors here, and the church family."

Stewart nodded soberly. Ed and his wife probably had hoped to be near their grandchildren when they retired, the same as he and Connie had. But the way things were going for the Harding and Wallace families, grandchildren might be a long time coming.

"How are the girls?"

"Fine," Ed replied. "Wynne's working for a little weekly newspaper. It's not much, and she'd like to move up to a daily. Rebecca's still at the hospital in Portland."

"Good." Stewart didn't think he should probe further.

"Say, how's Rob doing?" Ed asked, as though his thoughts had traveled the same path.

Stewart hesitated. "I guess he's all right, but I'd like to see him a little more enthusiastic about living."

Ed frowned. "Sorry to hear that. Rob's such a bright young man."

"Well, maybe that's a drawback sometimes. Some days I think he might be happier milking cows or pumping gas." Stewart shrugged, looking down at his clipboard. "We're proud of him, but I'm not sure we can help him out of this slump."

"Did he ever tell you what-all happened between him and Rebecca?" Immediately Ed held up one hand in apology. "Sorry. It's not my business, I know. But we've been stymied by Rebecca's attitude. It had to more than just the waiting. But I have no right to ask."

Stewart sighed. "Kids. The heartache we go through for them! I think Rob just assumed things would go the way he pictured them, but he didn't bother to consult Rebecca before he accepted that job in Brazil." He shook his head. "Looking back, he probably should have turned that down."

"Hindsight."

"Yeah. If I could fix things between them, I surely would, but it's been a long time now, and I don't see any change on that front."

"Me either. Just wishful thinking, I guess. Becca won't even talk to us about him, even after all this time."

It bothered Stewart deeply to think Rob had done something to hurt Ed's daughter so badly. "We love her. Always figured she'd be part of the family."

"We felt the same about Rob." Ed exhaled heavily. "I'd better get my things and go back to the house. Long drive home tonight." He met Stewart's gaze, his eyes full of anxiety. "I know you and Connie must pray for Rob constantly."

Stewart nodded. "He and Debbie take up a lot our prayer time."

"I thought Debbie was getting married."

"Well, she's had some problems too. Things are on ice for now, and we're hoping she'll call it off permanently."

Ed's eyebrows arched. "I'm sorry she's had a tough time."

"Yes, well, she deserves better." Stewart smiled contritely. "Listen to us. We've got great kids, but all we do is complain. I'm surprised that Rebecca is still single, though. She was always such a bright spot. I figured when she broke up with Rob, some other fellow would snap her up quick."

"There hasn't been another man in her life, at least not that we've heard about. She's not the same girl now. Would you pray for Rebecca too?"

"Of course." Stewart put out his hand and they shook once more.

❧❧❧

Brittany invited two other women to have lunch with her on Thursday. In Rob's absence, her workdays dragged interminably, and lunch hours were flat and boring. She'd been filling them with shopping all week, but her credit card balances were near the maximum, and she decided she'd better not spend any more until she got her next paycheck.

As she and her friends stepped out into the hot sunshine, she saw a young blond man getting out of a pickup truck in the firm's parking lot.

"Hunk alert," hissed Erin, the file clerk.

"I'll say," Brittany agreed automatically, sizing up the fellow. He was wearing a chambray shirt and black jeans, and his hair was a little unruly, but he was definitely attractive. He stood looking the three of them over frankly as they headed for Erin's car. Brittany walked a little slower and let her eyes lock his as a half-smile formed on her expertly made up lips.

He smiled back, and she could see that he was going to speak to them. Brittany felt alive, ready for anything. If he was vulgar, she would cut him down to size. And if he was nice, well, she was confident, and she was almost never at a loss for words when talking to a man.

"Excuse me." He slouched lazily against the door of his truck, and the trio of women stopped and looked at him. "Would any of you ladies happen to know Rob Wallace? I understand he works here."

Erin chuckled. "That's your department, Brit." She and Kayla moved toward the car, and Brittany took a step toward the man. Rob certainly had good taste in friends. It figured. One gorgeous guy would hang out with another.

"I know Rob," she said easily, letting her eyelashes sweep downward. "He's not here today, though."

"Oh." The man's eyes darkened. "That's too bad. I was in town, and I was hoping to connect with him. He's not sick, is he? I drove past his folks' house, but there was nobody home."

Brittany's mind was whizzing. "You know Rob's family?"

"Yeah, I do. We're old friends."

"Well, Rob's on vacation this week."

"Oh. Well, maybe I can catch up with his sister. Do you know Debbie?"

"No. He's mentioned her once or twice, but I've never met her."

Kayla rolled down the window of Erin's Tercel and called, "Are you coming, Brittany?"

She looked at the man speculatively, then raised her eyebrows just a bit, smiling.

"Say, I know this is a bit presumptuous," the man said with a grin, "but I'm starved. How about having lunch with a friend of a friend?"

She hesitated for just a fraction of an instant. Why not? Rob had deserted her voluntarily for ten days. It would serve him right if she made some time with his good-looking buddy. She could dangle it in front of him when he came back to work.

Too bad you missed your friend. He insisted on buying me lunch.
Maybe it would do Rob good to feel a pang or two of jealousy.

"All right." She turned toward the car. "Go ahead," she
called, and Kayla looked at Erin, then shrugged and rolled up
the window.

"I'm Brittany Dexter." She stepped toward him as Erin's car
left the lot.

"Mark Elliott."

They shook hands. His grip was firm, and he had a deep
tan, although it was early in the season. Brittany smiled up into
his blue eyes, and Mark gave her another crooked grin. "How
well do you know old Rob?"

"We're pretty close," she admitted.

"That right?" He was taking in every detail of her outfit. She
dressed professionally for work, but with what she called a dash
of pizzazz. The new suit she was wearing had a shorter skirt
than she'd been wearing lately. She'd decided to try it out
before Rob came back, as he tended to be a bit stodgy when it
came to fashion. She'd feared old Mr. Hanson would send her a
memo about the dress code, but it hadn't happened. On the
contrary, he'd smiled at her in the elevator with an interest that
was less fatherly than his usual look.

"So, you know a good place to eat and get acquainted?"
Mark asked.

"I sure do." She eyed the dark pickup truck dubiously.
"Care to ride in my RX7?"

She headed for an upscale restaurant that she knew her coworkers wouldn't patronize during the lunch hour. Mark's eyes
glittered as he visually explored the car on the way, and she
laughed.

"Like it?"

"I sure do."

"What's your other car?" she asked.

He grinned. "A Ferrari."

Brittany's laugh rippled out. She could tell he was lying,
and that he knew she knew, and it was fun. This guy wasn't

nearly so straight-laced as Rob. Maybe she'd have a date this weekend, after all.

They lingered over the buffet lunch, and Brittany broke her stringent diet for dessert. It was a day of indulgence. She was already planning how she'd explain the extra-long lunch hour she was stealing.

"You know," she said, licking her lips after a bite of cheesecake, knowing how tempting she looked, "I just thought of a place where you might find Rob."

Mark was immediately interested. "I thought he was out of town."

"Well, not exactly. He's got a camp on Messalonskee Lake. Have you ever been there?" She waited, her heart tripping rapidly.

"No, I guess I didn't know about that. Hey!" He looked up hopefully. "Do you think Debbie would be there?"

"Well, I don't know," Brittany said thoughtfully, although Rob had made it clear he was going to the cottage alone. Mark was obviously as interested in finding Debbie as he was in finding Rob. "I'm pretty sure Rob was planning to spend the week there. I guess it's possible his sister went with him."

"So, how do I find it?"

She smiled ruefully. "That's a good question. I've never been there, either."

Mark shrugged a little, sipping his second beer. "It wouldn't be that hard to find, I guess."

"No?"

"You said it's in Belgrade, right?"

"I'm pretty sure."

Mark nodded. "The town office will have maps showing all the lot owners."

Brittany sat back, chiding herself for not thinking of that. She worked with real estate records all the time. She could have gone to the Belgrade town office and looked weeks ago. The maps were public record.

"You're a pretty smart guy." She gave him her most alluring smile. "Sneaky, but smart." She lifted her wine glass.

"So, what are my chances of seeing you again?" Mark asked. "How smart do I have to be to do that?"

"Oh, I think you're right up there in the brilliant category." She took a sip. The air between them was charged with suppressed energy. "I'd better get back to work, but I think we definitely want to continue this." She opened her purse and took out a business card, writing quickly on the back. "Here's my cell phone number. I don't give it out to just anyone."

Mark sat back, his disarming smile cutting right through all pretense. "But since I'm such a good friend of Rob's ..."

She nodded. "I think you're smart enough to call me tonight. I'll be interested to know if you catch up with your friend."

Chapter 13

Rob was going through his tackle box on the screened-in porch on Friday afternoon when he heard a car coming down the gravel camp road. *It must be Dad,* he thought. His parents and Pastor Fields were the only ones he'd told the exact location of the cottage. He got up and went to the door, hoping nothing was wrong at home. To his surprise, the pastor was getting out of his sedan.

"Hey, Pastor," he called. "What's up?"

Mr. Fields smiled and strolled toward him, looking around at the pleasant, shaded lot and the lake, a placid steel blue today.

"Rob, I'm sorry if I'm interrupting anything, but I've been thinking about you all week." He stopped a few feet away and looked at Rob inquiringly.

"No, that's fine," Rob assured him. "I was just sorting my tackle and thinking about going out fishing later."

"Sounds great."

"Come on in," Rob said.

"You sure? I know you said emergencies only."

Rob shrugged. "Actually, I found I was talking to myself this morning. It's probably time I came out of seclusion again."

Pastor Fields laughed and followed him inside. "Beautiful location you've got here."

"Thanks. I've been thinking I ought to share it with more people. Coffee?" Rob asked.

"Sure."

They settled down at the porch table with their mugs, and Rob absently returned to arranging the lures and fishing flies.

"Missed you Sunday," the pastor said. "Your folks told me where you were, and I figured that was fine. You need some time away from the job. But somehow the Lord wouldn't let me get you out of my mind."

Rob smiled. "Have you been praying for me this week?"

"Almost constantly. Is something going on?"

Rob fingered the lead sinker in his hand and nodded. "You know me, pastor. I don't go asking for help very often. As usual, I've been trying to handle things on my own."

"Is it working?"

"Maybe. I've been praying a lot this week, too."

"Well, that's good."

"Mm. Well, I shouldn't have skipped church. I apologize."

"You don't have to apologize to me."

Rob picked up his coffee mug, then set it down again. "I've been convicted about the way I've behaved lately." He laughed without humor. "Who am I kidding? It's not just lately. I haven't been reading the Bible or praying regularly for a long time, but you knew that, didn't you?"

The pastor said, "Well, when a person doesn't come to services regularly for months on end, that's a pretty good indicator."

Rob nodded. "I haven't been on very good terms with the Lord."

"Why is that, Rob?"

He gritted his teeth, then sighed. "It started a long time ago. I got angry. I let it fester. I knew it wasn't right."

"You were blaming God for something?"

"Not exactly. But I figured He could help me straighten things out. I asked Him to, but things got worse."

The pastor was quiet for a moment. "You've been lonely."

Rob nodded. "Ever since Rebecca broke up with me."

"We all figured you two would get married," the pastor said softly. "I'm sorry it didn't work out, Rob."

"Thanks. But the worst of it is, well, recently I started seeing a woman I work with, and ..." He eyed the pastor apprehensively, wondering how shocked he would be. "She's not a Christian."

Mr. Fields nodded. Rob waited, but the pastor just picked up one of the flies Rob's father had tied and examined it closely. "Blue Dunn," he said.

"Aren't you going to say anything?" Rob asked.

"What do you want me to say?"

"That I know better, maybe? That I haven't been obedient to God?"

"You already know that. Would it help you to hear it from me?"

Rob smiled then. "Why are you really here?"

The pastor shrugged. "To listen, maybe. Not to lecture you, certainly."

"You like to fish, don't you?" Rob asked.

"Well, yes."

"Have you got a license? I've got another pole in the shed."

The pastor stood up with a twinkle in his eye. "Now you're talking."

Half an hour later they were drifting near the brushy shore of the island, casting their lines to the edge of the overhanging branches near the rocks.

Rob reeled in his line slowly and glanced at the pastor under the brim of his baseball cap. "I think I've finally accepted it that Rebecca doesn't want me in her life anymore. I still love her, but if she doesn't love me, there's nothing I can do. And if God doesn't want us together, I need to quit wishing for that."

"Well, it's hard to let go of someone you hold dear." The pastor's face was sorrowful as he delicately landed a fly on the calm surface of the lake. "But you're probably right about that. You need to be open to whatever the Lord has for you, even if it's not the future you counted on."

"Yes, sir. It's taken me a long time, but I think I've settled that with God now."

The pastor pulled the slack out of his line. "And what about this other girl?"

Rob swallowed and laid his rod down in the bottom of the canoe. He sat in silence for a minute, watching the pastor bring his line in.

"Well, I know I've got to tell her as soon as I can, that's all. I wanted to do it last week, but I just couldn't get the words out."

"What will you say?" Mr. Fields asked.

"I'll tell her I'm sorry I let her think there could be a permanent relationship, and I'll make it clear that there can't be. It's obvious now that I can't keep seeing her and serve God."

"Maybe you should call her when you go back home."

Rob shook his head. "I need to tell her to her face. I think I owe her that."

The pastor shrugged. "Maybe so. Just be wary." His rod bent sharply and he grinned. "Hey! That's a big one! Get the net ready, Rob."

◖◍◗

It was nearly six o'clock when Mark drove down the rutted dirt road toward the lake. He'd left the construction site a bit early, to make sure he got to the town office before closing. The clerk there had been very obliging.

Mark cut the motor and rolled into an empty spot between Rob's car and another that he didn't recognize. It was very quiet, and he wasn't quite sure what to do, but he needed to know if Debbie was here. She'd stalled him long enough.

His bitterness grew as he thought about it. She was listening to her father again. Stewart had never liked him. Well, he wasn't prepared to let her just walk out of his life like that. It would be over when he said it was over. And even if he did say it was over, there was the matter of the diamond. It had cost him a bundle.

After a moment's thought, he walked boldly up to the cottage door and knocked. There was no response. He waited, knocked again, then ambled around the corner of the building.

104

Nice little place Rob had here. A deck chair sat on the dock below, and a swimming float was anchored farther out. Mark walked down onto the pier and looked out over the lake.

Northward, toward Oakland, he saw a canoe floating on the calm surface. Two people were sitting in it, fishing. He wished he had binoculars, but he was pretty sure one was Rob. And the other was definitely not Debbie. No, it was a man.

Mark nodded and turned away. Debbie's car wasn't here or at her parents' house. He'd dropped by her apartment and the medical building in Bangor early that morning, but she wasn't there, either. Maybe she'd taken a new job. Another lead played out.

He started his truck, wondering how he could pick up the scent again. Well, he wouldn't waste the whole weekend pining, that was for sure. Rob's sophisticated friend at work seemed more than willing to spend some time with him. He got the feeling she and Rob were pretty tight, but she'd been tense about the cottage. For whatever reason, Rob had kept the location from her. He'd just have to help her forget about it and unwind a notch or two.

Debbie thought a lot of her brother, but Mark had always considered Rob a bit of a fool. He was too quiet and serious, with no idea how to have fun. And no doubt he was taking Debbie's side now.

Mark had stopped by the architectural firm hoping to play on his sympathies a little, maybe get Rob to see things his way and convince him to put in a good word for him with Debbie, or at least give him a clue as to her whereabouts. But now that he'd met Brittany Dexter, Mark had no desire to buddy up to Rob.

It had become a test of wills with Debbie, and her family was his enemy in the contest. Mark had never really thought Rob would take his part, and he was certain Stewart was fuming. No doubt the restraining order had been his idea.

Needling the Wallace family in small ways might be gratifying, especially if he found ways to do it that wouldn't justify them calling in the cops. There was no law against dating

Debbie's brother's girlfriend. Yes, it would be satisfying to romance Rob's girl while he was off fishing.

Chapter 14

After his week in solitude, Rob felt rested and relaxed, less tense than he had in years. He packed up early Sunday morning and left the cottage in time to meet his parents and Debbie at church.

He waited in the parking lot until they drove in. As his father stepped out of the car, Rob approached him.

"Dad, maybe this should wait, but I need to tell you. I'm sorry for all the anxiety I put you and Mom through."

Stewart stared at him for a moment. Rob extended his hand tentatively, but his father broke into a grin and hugged him.

"Thank you, son. Everything straightened out now?"

"Yes. Well, there are a few things I have to take care of, but I know what I have to do now."

Stewart nodded. "Welcome back."

That night Rob went back to church with them for the evening service. His parents made no comment, but he could tell his mother was extremely happy.

"Did you eat that trout yet?" he asked Pastor Fields on the way out.

"Yes. My wife cooked it for supper Friday. Best fish I ever ate." He leaned closer. "Are you ready to deliver your message to that young woman?"

"Yes, sir. I'd appreciate it if you'd keep praying about it. It probably won't be easy."

After they got home, Rob sat on the chair swing in the back yard with Debbie, languidly sipping iced tea. "So, how's the new job going?" he asked.

"I like it." Her voice was eager, and that gave Rob some satisfaction. "It's not as challenging as the old one, but maybe that's good, at least for now. I need something fairly mindless for a while. Of course, the pay is less. A doctor's receptionist can't command the same salary a medical researcher gets."

"Did you meet a lot of new people?"

"Oh, tons of them. And I saw Laura Hendsbee. She brought her son in for shots. Does that make you feel old, or what?"

Rob winced. "Definitely. She's younger than you, isn't she?"

"A year." Debbie drained her glass. "I just hope Mark doesn't hear about it somehow and come find me at work again. I'm kind of surprised he hasn't come back here."

"Well, putting your car in the garage every night may be helping."

"Maybe he finally gave up."

Rob considered that. He didn't know Mark very well, but he knew he was stubborn. "Maybe." They sat in silence for several minutes.

"Do you think I should find an apartment in Waterville?" Debbie asked.

Rob sat up straighter and stared at her in the dusk. "Why? Mom and Dad are glad to have you home."

She shrugged. "I don't want to cause them any trouble."

"They'd worry about you if you moved out. Better stay here a while until we're sure things have settled down. Besides, it would cost a lot more to rent a place of your own."

She smiled. "Can't beat the price of the Wallace B&B, can we?"

The rising moon glinted on her glass, and he noticed suddenly that there was no flash from her finger. "You're not wearing your ring anymore."

"Nope. I figure it's over."

Rob nodded solemnly. "I've been praying for you all week."

She looked at him, wide-eyed. "Thanks. I've been praying, too. I haven't been doing enough of that lately."

"Me either. What Dad said at the cemetery—well, he was right about me."

"Me too. It feels good to be back on track spiritually, even though this business with Mark feels awful."

"I know what you mean." Rob slouched comfortably on the swing.

"I missed you this week."

"Same here." They sat in silence, and Rob rocked the swing back and forth slowly.

"Did Becca send it back?" Debbie asked as the darkness thickened.

"What?"

"Her ring. Did she send it back when you broke up?"

Rob shifted and brought his right foot up to rest on his knee. "No."

Debbie nodded and pushed the swing again.

"I told her to keep it," he offered a minute later.

"Oh. Because I don't know what to do with mine. I guess I could mail it back. He hasn't told me to keep it or anything like that."

"You haven't told him you don't want it anymore, have you?"

She sighed. "Technically, no. Do I have to? I mean, I just don't want to talk to him again. At all." She peered at him hopefully. "Maybe you or Dad could take it back to him."

"Maybe you could send it registered mail," Rob countered.

"Yeah, maybe."

Behind them, the kitchen light went out.

"Mom and Dad are going to bed," Rob noted. "Guess we should too."

"How long does it hurt?" Debbie asked.

Rob took a deep breath. "Do you still love him?"

She hesitated. "I'm not sure."

"Guess it will be a while, then."

"Do you still love Becca?"

He didn't want to answer. He kept pushing the swing, and the question hung between them. Finally he said softly, "Let me put it this way: it still hurts."

❧❦❧

Rob went back to work eager to delve into a new project. He and Eric were working together to design a new municipal building for the town of Skowhegan and would spend most of Monday with the town officials in that town, discussing the needs the new building would meet.

Brittany greeted him coolly when he came back to the office after lunch. He hadn't seen her in the morning, but her radar must have been up when he and Eric returned. She found him in the copier room less than five minutes after he'd walked through the door.

"Well, well. Did you have a nice vacation?"

"Yes, I did. It was very restful." He stacked the papers he was copying.

She waited. Apparently she expected more, but this wasn't the time to tell her the conclusion he had reached.

"I feel much better," he said. "Sat in the sun, did a little fishing. How was your week?"

"Interesting," was her cryptic reply. "So, listen, I have an invitation for Friday night, but I wasn't sure if you wanted to do something this week." Her voice was quieter than usual, almost timid.

"Go ahead," he said. "I was planning to go back to the cottage for the weekend, anyway." She looked a little disappointed, even though she was the one who had other plans. He said, "But we really need to talk soon, Brittany. There are things we should discuss."

She brightened. "How about Wednesday?"

"I don't think so." He took a deep breath. "Unless you want to go to church with me."

"Church? On a weekday?"

"Yes. We could have dinner first."

110

She grimaced. "No, thanks. Do you have plans for lunch tomorrow?"

"Yes, I do. I've got to meet with a client. I'll be tied up most of the afternoon."

Brittany frowned. "Well, I don't know when we can get together, then, Rob. I'm very busy, and you seem to have your weekends planned."

"We'll work something out." Maybe he could just tell her now. She seemed willing to loosen the bond a little, and she didn't sound angry with him for being tightly scheduled. He was about to suggest that they should remain casual friends when Mr. Hanson came to the doorway of the copier room.

"There you are, Brittany. Do you have that estimate on the Fairfax job?"

"Yes, sir. I'll bring it to your office right away."

The boss nodded and left, and Brittany edged toward the door.

"Just let me know when you have a free evening, Rob."

"Sure." He gathered his papers and headed for his office, surprised that it had been that easy. His old aversion to confrontation was satisfied. If he could stave it off long enough, he might not ever have to have that difficult conversation with Brittany.

In fact, with her outgoing personality, she would get tired of waiting around and find someone else. Within a month she would forget about him, he was certain. He felt suddenly free, and he laughed aloud.

"What's funny?" Eric asked from the doorway.

"Nothing. I just feel good."

His friend eyed him cautiously. "You didn't pop the question with Brit, did you?"

"Far from it." Rob smiled and sat down at his desk, but somehow it didn't feel quite right. *Lord, she doesn't care,* he prayed silently. *Isn't this enough?* Something told him that once again he was fooling himself.

Chapter 15

Rebecca went to work each day seeking opportunities to help her patients spiritually. She didn't have much of a chance to witness to her coworkers, other than Faye, but a quiet word now and then told the other nurses that she took her faith seriously.

On days when she was charge nurse, she found herself combing the other nurses' charts and charge slips carefully. Several times she pointed out mistakes and overcharges, and it didn't win her any friends. Stacy in particular seemed to resent her manner.

"It's a philosophical difference," Stacy said archly.

"But it doesn't make sense to charge for more than we need to," Rebecca argued.

"It doesn't hurt the patient."

"But it doesn't benefit the patient, either. And it doesn't benefit you." Rebecca shook her head in exasperation. "Just use common sense, Stacy. Think about each item that you bill for. Hilda has been on my case about this lately, and I'm trying to be conscientious about it."

"Sure," Stacy said stonily, walking away.

Rebecca planned to take her vacation the second and third weeks in July. It was hot, even on Casco Bay, and she could hardly wait to get out of Portland. The city was steaming. Tourists overran the area, and the hospital emergency room was always full.

She wished she knew if Rob had stayed at the cottage for the whole month of June. It would be easy for him to commute to Waterville from the lake. If only she could do that! But the ninety-minute drive each way was not her idea of an easy commute to work.

She went to visit her parents over the Fourth of July. It was odd to have a Thursday off, and she wished she had the Friday, too. She would have raced up to Belgrade and installed herself on the lakeshore early. But she didn't have it off, so she drove to the family's new home and played horseshoes with her father and badminton with her sister. They ate grilled chicken and potato salad and listened to her mother's nonstop updates on the family.

"Do you hear anything from Rob?" her father asked over dessert. They all sat in lawn chairs, under a huge maple, licking ice cream cones.

Rebecca shook her head. "We don't talk, Dad."

"Pity."

She sighed. Occasionally her father brought up the subject, and inevitably she left feeling guilty.

"Are you going to church up there?" her mother asked.

"I'll probably go to that one in Augusta, where Faye and I visited in May."

"You ought to go back to the old church," her father chided. "Just because you don't want to see Rob, doesn't mean you can't go to your old church."

"Yes," her mother agreed. "Lots of people there would like to see you. Pastor Fields, for instance. And Elsie might be home for the summer."

Rebecca sighed. She and Elsie Fields had been good friends in high school. She would like to see some of her old friends, it was true. But not at the risk of seeing Rob.

"I'll think about it."

"Hey," her sister said. "How about another game of badminton?"

"You're on." Rebecca was thankful Wynne had ended the conversation, but she knew she would think about it, as she'd promised.

SOCS

She arrived at the cottage early Friday evening, before eight o'clock, and unloaded her supplies. She opened the refrigerator, half expecting to find a moldy quart of strawberries. Instead, there was a six-pack of Diet Pepsi. When she opened the little freezer above, she found a quart of peppermint ice cream. She couldn't hold back her smile. He remembered, after all this time. She found herself humming as she put away the groceries.

She took her bags upstairs and found the bedroom immaculate, with the double bed made up fresh. Rob had done that before, at the end of his own time in residence, but something seemed different this time.

Then she knew. An afghan of blue blocks, crocheted in different shades, was folded at the end of the bed. It looked brand new, but she knew it was three and a half years old. She had put every stitch into it with eager love. She touched it with her fingertips. It was softer than she remembered. Maybe Connie had washed it in Downy.

What did it mean? Maybe Rob never used it at home, so he'd relegated it to the cottage with the chipped plates and discarded silverware. Or had he brought it to remind him of the more pleasant past? And why had he left it here now? Had he meant for her to find it, inducing guilt? Nostalgia? Regret?

The sun was down behind the tree line, and a cool breeze came off the lake. She pulled on a sweatshirt and took the path to the shore. Rob had left the canoe tied up at the dock, and she knew when she saw it that he had been there that day. He wouldn't go off and leave the canoe out for several days with no one in the cottage. She understood, too, that he had left it out for her, so she could use it without struggling to carry it to the shore.

She heard a car on the gravel lot above, and turned toward it, her pulse quickening. Rob wouldn't come see her. Would he?

A low silver sports car glided to a stop beside her compact, and a woman got out. Rebecca began walking slowly up the path, trying to see something familiar in the shape and movement of the young woman, but she couldn't place her.

"Oh, hello," the stranger said uncertainly when she saw Rebecca. She'd been headed toward the front door, but she veered toward the lake path instead, and met Rebecca near the corner of the cottage.

"May I help you?" Rebecca asked. The woman was strikingly pretty, with pale blonde hair that couldn't be natural and vivid blue eyes.

"I was looking for someone," she purred. "I guess I've got the wrong cottage."

"Who did you want?" Rebecca asked, taking in the sleek white slacks that fit her curves to perfection, and the green silk blouse that gave her a sophisticated, yet alluring look.

"Uh, R-Richard Smith." The blonde smiled ingenuously. "He's my uncle. He and Aunt Sophie invited me for the weekend." It came out in a rush.

Rebecca realized the woman was sizing her up, and she felt suddenly scruffy in her sweatshirt and jeans. "I don't know the Smiths." She racked her brain to remember the names of the people who owned the nearest cottages.

The blonde shrugged. "Likely I got the wrong road. Is this 42?"

"No, it's Fire Road 45."

The flawless brow cleared. "There. You see? I got it wrong. Aunt Sadie will be so amused when I tell her. Sorry to bother you." She turned and walked quickly back toward her car.

Rebecca watched her, trying silently to analyze the wariness and hurt that leaped inside her. There was nothing innocent about her visitor.

When she went back inside and started the fire in the hearth, it didn't take her long to spot the new books Rob had

116

left. There were several new mysteries. She wrinkled her nose at the gory covers. She saw enough blood at the hospital.

But there was also a book on prayer. That was new. She pulled it down thoughtfully. What was Rob saying to her, if anything? His name was inside the cover, in his bold, tilted writing.

She leafed through it and saw several passages highlighted. She swallowed hard and laid it on the sofa. Maybe she'd read some tomorrow, to see what parts Rob had felt were important. He probably had a strong, vibrant prayer life, while she was just getting hers back on track after more than three years. She remembered how they had prayed together while they were dating. She had lost so much since then, but now, with God's help, she was regaining the ground.

One of her own books was lying on the twig end table. She picked it up and saw a small piece of paper sticking out. Her name was printed in his backward-slanting hand. Her adrenaline surged. She pulled the paper from the Boyden diary and read, *Becca, thanks for leaving this. I enjoyed reading it. Enjoy your time here. RW.*

She took a shaky breath and closed her eyes, not sure she could deal with Rob making tiny inroads on her life from a distance.

She went to the kitchen and put a kettle of water on the stove, then headed for the bathroom. In the doorway, she froze. Hanging on a hook in the corner by the hot water heater was a red plaid flannel shirt.

Her hands trembled as she took it and held it to her face. She breathed in the faint scent of him, and the tears came unbidden. She pulled the soft shirt on over her T-shirt. The sleeves were far too long, so she folded the cuffs back and wrapped the loose front around her. Had he grown since she'd seen him, or had she just forgotten how tall and comfortably large he was?

The teakettle whistled, and she hurried to take it off the burner then sat on the screened porch with her cup of tea, hugging the flannel shirt around her. She wore it all evening, but took it off before heading up to bed, reluctantly hanging it back where she had found it. This line of thinking would only reopen the old wounds.

In the middle of the night she was still awake, knowing it was too late. The wounds ached painfully.

◖◗◖◗

The first week was uneventful, and she pampered herself, sleeping late and lazing in the sun. On the calmest days she canoed, and she swam every day. She went through two bottles of sunscreen. The fresh air and change of pace caught up with her, and she slept soundly after that first restless night, for nine hours at a stretch.

On Sunday she put on a cotton dress and sandals and drove to the church in Augusta. She would really have liked to go to the service at her family's home church, but the fear of running into Rob and his parents there kept her away. As much as she would love to see Pastor and Mrs. Fields and Elsie, and even Connie and Stewart Wallace, she couldn't bring herself to brave the probability of meeting Rob face to face.

She drove into town on Monday, to use the Laundromat and call her parents. The reception on her phone was much better here than out at the lake.

"Just wanted you to know I'm still alive," she said with a laugh when her mother answered.

"Take care, dear. You hear so many stories these days."

"I'm fine, Mom."

"You shouldn't stay up there alone."

"It's less dangerous than staying alone in my apartment in Portland. How are things in New Hampshire?"

"It's been awfully hot."

Rebecca felt a stab of guilt. It had been warm, but not oppressive, on the lake. She ought to have invited her folks to come up.

"Do you and Dad want to come up and visit?"

118

"No, you're having your quiet time. Besides, the garden is coming on fast."

"You don't need to can a million jars of food anymore, Mom."

"I hate to let it go to waste."

"You never change." Rebecca laughed. "Are you making jam, too?"

"Naturally. Extra blackberry for you, dear."

"Thanks. I love you." Rebecca signed off and put her clothes in the dryer. Her watch had stopped. She decided to walk down the block to the jewelry store for a new battery while the laundry cycled.

Her stomach fluttered as she approached the store. She hadn't been in since they had bought her engagement ring here. She stopped on the sidewalk and looked at the window display without seeing it, waiting for her nerves to settle, but they refused. She gulped a big breath and decided to skip it. She'd run into Wal-Mart for the battery, after the laundry was done.

As she turned away from the window, her heart lurched. She had forgotten the architectural firm's building was so close, just across the street. Hanson Associates. The building looked modern, but classic at the same time, and the grounds were impeccably maintained.

She wondered what sort of office Rob had, and if he was happy there. She had expected him to take a job with a larger firm, in Boston, maybe, after he finished graduate school, since their plans had been shattered. But he'd come back here, near his folks and the cottage. She was the one who had cut herself adrift, living alone in a tiny apartment two hours from her parents, far from all her old friends.

People streamed out the doors of Hanson Associates. It must be noon. She glanced futilely at her watch, remembering the purpose of her errand. The last thing she wanted was to see Rob. Or was it?

She blinked. A blonde had emerged from the office building with another woman. The blonde looked suspiciously like the one who'd come to the cottage and claimed to be lost. Rebecca dived into the jewelry store.

When she got back to the cottage, she put her laundry away and took the Waterville newspaper she'd bought down to the dock. She scanned the headlines quickly and turned to the local section. The Belgrade selectmen had a disagreement over a proposed ordinance. She recognized the chairman's name; she had gone to school with his daughter. A new building supply was going into the plaza in Waterville. That might hurt Stewart Wallace's business.

She turned the page and looked at the photo at the top. It couldn't be. She sat forward and devoured the caption. It was Rob, all right, with two of Skowhegan's city councilmen. His firm was designing a new municipal building, and Rob was head architect on the project.

She stared at the photo for a long time. It was black and white, a little grainy. The elevation drawing of the new building was the focal point of the photograph, not Rob, but it was still enough to leave her feeling steamrollered.

He was better looking than ever, with an air of confidence and professionalism. That was her Rob, but better, if possible. Her breath whooshed out. Now that she'd seen what he looked like these days, she could no longer deny her remorseful loneliness. He would never be her Rob again, and it was her own fault. What had she done?

Lord, I've got to get over this! You've got to take these feelings away, or fifty years from now I'll be a white-haired spinster still mourning for Rob.

Chapter 16

When the Wallaces returned from Bible study Wednesday evening, the phone was ringing. Rob grabbed the receiver from the wall phone in the kitchen, laying his Bible on the countertop.

"Rob, is that you?"

"Yes." He couldn't quite place the woman's voice.

"It's Myra Harding. How are you doing?"

Rob stood stock still. Rebecca's mother. His heartbeat accelerated on principle.

"I—I'm fine, Mrs. Harding. How are you?"

"So formal," she chided. "I'm doing all right, but Ed and I wondered if you could do us a favor."

"You name it," he said quickly.

"Could you get a message to Rebecca at the cottage?"

His heart plummeted. Well, he'd laid himself wide open for that.

"Sure. Of course. I didn't realize she was staying up here this week."

"Yes, it's her vacation. She's due home Sunday."

"Is everything all right?" he asked. Connie had come into the kitchen and was watching him with worried eyes.

"Yes, it's just that her cousin Terri is here from California. Rebecca hasn't seen her in years, and I thought she might like to come down before Terri goes back. She doesn't need to rush it. If she left early Sunday and drove down here, she could spend half a day with the family."

"She'd probably like that," Rob said.

"Well, it's not urgent, but I wasn't sure she'd get the message in time if I wrote, and her cell phone doesn't seem to work down on the lake. You don't need to drive over there tonight or anything."

Rob swallowed. "I'll go tomorrow, then." He wondered if Rebecca would let him through the door.

"Thank you, son."

He was afraid she was going to hang up, and he didn't want the conversation to end yet. "Is Ed all right?"

"Yes, he's fine. How about your folks?"

"Everybody's good here."

"I'm glad. We've been praying for you."

He swallowed. "Thank you. We miss having you in the neighborhood."

"Ask Rebecca to call me if she's not coming, would you, Rob?"

"Of course."

He hung up and stood staring at the phone for a long minute. He turned around and found his mother's eyes still on him, but she said nothing.

"Mrs. Harding," he said tightly. "They need me to take a message to Rebecca tomorrow."

"Do you want me to go?" Connie asked.

"No, it's all right. I'll go."

"No one's ill, I hope?"

"No. Just out-of-town relatives they want her to see."

He went up to his room, meeting Debbie in the hall.

"Why so glum?" she asked, smiling.

"I have to go see Rebecca tomorrow. Her mom called with a message."

Debbie's demeanor changed immediately. "Are you up for that?"

A short chuckle that was almost a moan came out. "I think ... I think I'll ask her if I can buy out her share of the cottage."

"Whoa."

Rob looked at his sister defensively. "What? You don't think I should?"

"Does she want to sell?"

"Not that I know of."

"So, you just want to get her name off the deed, or what?"

He sighed. "Not really. It's just so awkward. People don't understand."

"Does that matter?"

He shrugged. "I've been telling myself for three years that it doesn't."

"Then why does it matter now, all of a sudden?"

"I guess ... because Eric's been telling me how weird it is and because ..."

Debbie raised her eyebrows.

"Because now I have to go see her. I know I'm the last person in the world she wants to see."

"I can go if you'd rather. I could run over before I leave for work in the morning."

"No." It came out quickly, and he shrugged. "I can do it."

Debbie nodded slowly. "Pray about this, Rob."

❧◆❧

On Thursday, Rebecca took a Diet Pepsi and one of Rob's John Grisham novels to the dock and sat in a deck chair, reading. The plot was complicated, and she was having trouble keeping the characters straight. Maybe her mind was elsewhere. She laid the book down and looked out over the water. Gentle waves lapped the dock pilings. A boat pulling two water skiers hummed far down the lake, and near the island a seagull glided low over the surface of the water.

A noise behind her startled her, and she looked up toward the cottage. A man was coming down the path, and she rose quickly, her heart hammering as she recognized him.

"Hi, Becca." He stopped ten feet from her.

"Rob." It barely came out.

"You look great," he said.

She swallowed and wished she had on her white shorts, instead of her ragged denim cutoffs. He looked fabulous, but she couldn't say that. More mature, of course, but more handsome than the picture, even. He was tanned and muscular, and his hair ruffled in the breeze. He wore a blue cotton dress shirt and an eye-catching necktie, with gray slacks.

"Shouldn't you be at work?" she managed.

"I'm on my lunch hour."

She nodded. So he wouldn't be staying long. She looked him over again, not knowing what to say, finding it hard just to breathe normally.

"Your mom called."

Her eyes snapped to his. "Is something wrong?"

"No, but your cousin is visiting, and she thought you might want to drive down Sunday."

"Oh."

"She asked you to call her if you can't come."

"I'll call her anyway," Rebecca said. "I'll go into town this afternoon and call her."

"Great." He stood there uncertainly.

"Sit down," she invited, then realized there was only one deck chair. "Hey, did you eat? Because I've got sandwich stuff in the fridge. I can make you a sandwich like that." She snapped her fingers.

His smile came out then, the old, heart-stopping smile that always grabbed her and turned her inside out.

"Thanks. That would be nice."

She walked past him, careful not to get too close. They went in through the screened porch that faced the lake. "So, ham and cheese?" she asked, trying to sound normal, whatever that was anymore. Her thoughts and feelings were roiling, but she managed to stay outwardly calm.

"That'd be good."

She didn't look at him as she pulled the fixings from the refrigerator and prepared the sandwich. He leaned against the counter, watching. She didn't have to ask him how he liked it, she just spread the mayonnaise and added a tiny bit of mustard.

She grabbed a bag of barbecue potato chips from the cupboard. "No Dr. Pepper. Sorry."

"That's okay." His lopsided smile made her heart flip-flop.

"Iced tea?" She knew he didn't like Diet Pepsi.

"Sure."

She poured two glasses, and Rob picked them up.

"Where are we going?" he asked.

"The porch?"

She carried his plate and the chips to the screened porch, and he brought the drinks. Rob sat down facing the water, and Rebecca sat at the end of the table beside him. She was gratified when he bowed his head silently for a moment. He was still praying. She had guessed that after she'd found the book. She'd read it from cover to cover and found it helpful. Maybe he hadn't gone through any of the spiritual trauma she'd experienced.

He smiled and picked up half the sandwich. "Thanks. This is nice." He took a bite. He watched her while he chewed, and Rebecca found it difficult to sit still.

"So, chips?"

"No, thanks."

She opened the bag and pulled out a handful, more from nervousness than hunger. She ate several handfuls while Rob worked on the sandwich, then she realized she hadn't given him a paper napkin and jumped up to get one.

"Can I get you anything else? I've got yogurt and cream rolls."

He smiled. "You don't look as if you have even a nodding acquaintance with pastries."

"It's my dark secret."

He laughed. "You always ate like a horse and didn't gain weight."

"No longer true. I'm only indulging in junk food because it's my vacation."

He sipped his iced tea, then met her gaze. "I wanted to ask you something."

She waited, unable to hazard what could be important to him after all this time, where she was concerned. On the other hand, there were a million things she'd like to ask him.

Rob cleared his throat and looked down at his plate. "I was wondering if ... I don't know how to put this. Could I buy you out?"

Rebecca stared at him. "You mean ... the cottage?"

"Yes."

Her disappointment was almost crushing. So that was why he had been so nice, left her treats and offered the use of the canoe. He was buttering her up for this.

She stood and went to stand by the screened windows, looking out at the sun-splashed water. "I don't know what to say."

"I just thought maybe you were ready. I can afford to pay you your share of the down payment, and the monthly payments you've made, too, if you like."

For several seconds she stood silent, knowing that if she spoke she would cry. He must know her better than that, must realize that the cottage was part of her now. It had been their dream, but now it was her refuge. But he was all business, so she framed her reply. *I don't want to sell.* It was as simple as that.

Before she could swallow the lump in her throat and say it, she heard his chair move and sensed him standing close behind her. She stood still, barely breathing.

"It's an awkward arrangement, Becca," he said softly.

"It's worked for us."

"Has it? I thought maybe it was time ... to let go."

"Why?"

She whirled to face him and was startled by his nearness. She could touch him so easily. More than anything, she wanted to. She had to will her hands to stay at her sides. His soft brown eyes were fixed tenderly on her, and she couldn't believe he felt nothing toward her. They'd shared too much. As she looked at his face, so dear, so much a part of her life, something cold inside her began to melt.

126

He looked away first.

"Are *you* ready to let go?" she whispered hoarsely.

He shrugged helplessly, his eyes evading hers. "I just ... I thought it might be better to end this."

"To end what? We don't have anything left between us."

"I know." His voice was brittle. "I meant the cottage, the mortgage payments, the headaches."

Her brain swirled in confusion. "It's a headache for you?"

"Well, not so much that, but it kind of nags at me, you know?" His brown eyes were sorrowful, she thought, but then, could she really read his moods anymore? This offer had certainly been out of the blue.

"You want to just sell it, or you want it yourself?" She wished she could make a counter offer to buy his half, but she lived from paycheck to paycheck, struggling to pay the rent and keep her car running.

"I'd really like to hang onto it," Rob said. "I enjoy being here in the summer."

And I'm in the way. He wanted the cottage, obviously, but he wanted to be rid of her. She was the awkward part of his life now. *There must be a girl. Maybe he's getting married and wants to bring his bride here.*

"Let me think about it," she said stiffly.

"All right. How long?"

She knew she didn't really want to think about it, but he was forcing her hand. "Give me a couple of days?"

"Sure."

He turned toward the door. She followed him and closed it when he was gone, leaning against it, breathing deeply. There *must* be someone else. He wanted the cottage for his future family, and she was an embarrassment.

The shock of seeing him assailed her then, and she began to tremble. She hugged her arms and fought against the tears. It was a losing battle. She took a wobbly step toward the living room. She would curl up on the sofa and have a good cry, then she would think about his offer dispassionately.

There was a soft rap at the door and she whipped around. Through the glass window, she saw him peering in at her apologetically. Slowly she reached out and opened the door.

"Hi. Sorry, I forgot to give you this. My mother—" He held out a pint jar of raspberry jam, his eyes avoiding hers.

"She knew you were coming?"

"Yes. She asked me to say hello." He looked straight at her then. "Becca, are you all right?"

She realized her tears had betrayed her. She drew herself up to her full five-feet-four, but he still towered ten inches over her. "I'm fine." She held his gaze, determined to stare him down again, but a tiny sob escaped her.

"Becca!" His arms were around her, and she couldn't stand that. He was too solicitous, too warm, too tender. For almost four years she had been without his embrace. To have it now for a few seconds was torture.

She tried to pull away, but he held her firmly, with her head against his chest. She rested the jar of jam against his sleeve and wept, embarrassed and relieved at the same time. The sobs wracked her, and she clenched her fingers around his impeccable executive necktie. She'd bought him a tie once, when they were in college. It had Bugs Bunny on it.

"Here." He fumbled in his pocket and came out with a clean handkerchief. Always the gentleman. "Do you want to talk about it?"

She sniffed and shook her head. "Just go away again, please."

Slowly he unwrapped his arms and stood away from her. She felt cold in the midsummer sun. His poor shirt. Her tears had left damp blotches across the front of it, where he had cradled her head over his heart.

"Are you sure you're okay? I hate to leave you like this."

She couldn't stand the intensity of his direct stare any longer. Reaching for the edge of the door, she stepped back into the dimmer kitchen and made herself look away.

"Just go."

Chapter 17

"I know it's true, Rob. Why didn't you tell me?"

He sat facing Brittany across the table in the restaurant. He had hoped to avoid this meeting, dodging proposed lunch dates and evenings together, but in the end she had pressed him, and he knew it was inevitable. This would be their last date. If it killed him, he was going to end it tonight.

"The other owner is a woman," she said stonily. "Admit it."

"Yes." He felt better having said it, but Brittany pounced on it.

"Why couldn't you just tell me the simple truth, instead of making me dig it out of the musty old town records?"

"You went to the town office out in Belgrade?" he asked in disbelief.

She shrugged. "Not personally. Someone else did, and they told me about it."

That didn't make sense to Rob. "Who?"

She back-pedaled, and he thought a slight flush stained her cheeks, but maybe it was her blusher. All of her makeup was a little overdone.

"Just a guy I know. He went to look at the tax maps for something and saw your name on the lot, and he mentioned it to me. You and some woman. Why didn't you tell me?"

"It didn't seem important."

"Oh, sure. She was obviously important to you at some point."

He took a deep, slow breath and glanced around at the other diners, surprised no one was staring at them.

"We were engaged," he said quietly. "It's been over for a long time, but the cottage was just … a loose end. We both wanted to use it for vacations. Separate vacations. I haven't laid eyes on her for over three years. I swear."

"Three years?" Her doubt was obvious.

"Well, until yesterday."

Her expression went livid, and he winced. Why did he have to be such a stickler for accuracy?

"You're still seeing her."

"Once. I went to see her once, but only because her mother called and asked me to take her a message." Why did he have to explain anything to Brittany, anyway?

"She's staying there now." It was a statement of fact.

"Well, of course. It's—July is—is her month," he said feebly.

Brittany nodded sagely. "Oh, yes, her month. She gets May, July, and September. How could I have forgotten?"

Rob picked up his water glass and took a deep swallow. He was becoming entangled in Brittany's web once again, when he had imagined he was free. He mustn't let her drive him to responding out of guilt and anger. *Lord, I need You now,* he prayed silently. *I've never been able to handle her well on my own. You've got to help me do what's right.*

"I don't understand how you can claim your relationship with her is over, yet you insist on sharing a house with this woman for years. It's unconscionable!"

Rob looked around again, and this time the nearest couple was staring.

"Brittany, how many times do I have to say this? A., it's not a house. It's a camp, a cottage. B., you make it sound like Rebecca and I are at the cottage together, and we're not. Not ever. It's like a time share. What is so awful about that?"

Brittany glared at him. "When I break up with a man, I certainly don't keep the house."

He almost laughed but decided just in time that would be a mistake. "What do you suggest as an alternative?"

"If she won't sell out to you, then sell your share to someone else."

"I couldn't do that to her. She wouldn't be comfortable at all, going there and knowing strangers had it on the off months."

"Oh, you know her so well, and you're so concerned about her feelings," Brittany stormed. "You keep saying this thing is over, but I don't buy it for one second."

Rob inhaled deeply. "My relationship with her is over, but I want to keep my interest in the cottage. As a matter of fact, I've made her an offer. I'm just waiting for her to decide whether she wants to sell it to me."

"And then you'll sell it at a profit?"

He picked up his water glass and turned it slowly as he sent up another prayer for wisdom. "No, I want to keep it."

She stared at him. "You're letting this thing addle your brain. I saw the appraisal. You can make some money on it. Sell it and be done with it. Get rid of the past associations. For my sake, Rob. It's driving me crazy." She reached for his hand and stroked his long fingers, her tone softening.

"Brittany, this has nothing to do with you," he said, trying to keep his voice low.

"What concerns you concerns me."

"No. No, it doesn't."

"What are you saying?"

He took a deep breath. "I'm saying my personal life is none of your concern. I'm sorry if I've made you think otherwise, but I don't think we belong together."

She stared at him, her lips slightly parted, then looked toward the windows for a few seconds, obviously processing what he had said. When she turned back to him, he almost shivered. "Is that your way of telling me we have no future?"

"Yes, I guess it is. I should have told you earlier, but I honestly think we're wrong for each other. I've always believed in God, Brittany, and I want to do what's right."

She blinked. "I know you find going to church pleasant. I don't mind. Personally I find it boring, but if it makes you feel better—"

"That's not it. It's not about how it makes me feel."

"What is it, then? And what does this have to do with that adorable cottage?"

Rob's mind whirled. It was almost as if she'd seen the place, but that couldn't be. "Nothing. Not directly, anyhow. Brit, I go to church because my faith is important to me. I never made that clear to you, but I want to make it clear now. I want to obey God. I haven't been doing that. The Bible says Christians shouldn't have close relationships with people who don't trust in Christ."

"This isn't like you, Rob. What are you saying?"

"I can't see you anymore. Socially, I mean."

She raised her chin, and her eyes flashed. "We've been dating for more than four months. I can't believe you're treating me this way."

"I'm sorry. I should have said this sooner. I was attracted to you, and I didn't want to—" He glanced around. "Can we talk outside?"

"No, I want to hear what you have to say." She held him with her glacial blue eyes. "I've put a lot of hope into this relationship. Tell me it wasn't misplaced."

"Come on, Brittany. We haven't gone out in weeks. Don't tell me you've been sitting home alone weekends this past month. I know you better than that."

The look she fixed on him was poisonous. "I'm not the one at fault here."

"I'm sorry," he said again, feeling drained of strength. "I don't see this going anywhere good. I want to stop seeing you. Forgive me for not having the nerve to say that earlier. It's over."

The waitress came to the side of the table, smiling brightly. "Would you like dessert? We've got carrot cake and strawberry meringue today."

"No, thank you." Brittany pushed her chair back. "Rob, I think it's time you took me home."

∞∞

Rebecca didn't bother to drive to Waterville to call home. She found that reception was pretty good near the Belgrade town office, just a couple of miles up the road from the cottage. She got out of her car and leaned against the hood as she punched the buttons.

"Hey, Mom. I just wanted you to know I'll be down Sunday."

"Great. Terri's anxious to see you."

"Thanks for letting me know."

"You saw Rob?"

Rebecca hesitated. "Yeah. He came down to tell me."

"How is he?"

"Good."

"He sounded well."

"Yeah, he's—he's fine."

There was an awkward pause.

"Still got the cowlick?" her mother asked.

"No, I think he's got it tamed."

"He was always a good-looking boy."

"Well, he's no longer a boy, Mom."

"Still good looking, I'll bet."

Rebecca kicked at a pebble on the ground. It wasn't fair for her to blush when she couldn't even see the person she was talking to. "Well, yeah," she mumbled.

"Oh, come on, honey," her mother laughed. "I'm curious. On a scale of one to ten..."

"He's a twelve, all right? Now, leave me alone or I won't come home Sunday."

"I'm sorry. I shouldn't have teased you." There was sympathy in her mother's voice now. "Are you all right?"

"Yes."

133

Her mother hesitated. "Rebecca, forgive me. I guess deep down, I was hoping when Rob said he'd take that message that—well, you know."

"I think he has a girlfriend, Mom."

"Oh." The pause was deep.

A gorgeous, blond girlfriend who can't keep her aunts straight, Rebecca thought. "Listen, could you and Daddy pray for me?" Her voice trembled, and she hated that.

"Of course."

"Good." She wiped savagely at an errant tear. "I need to not feel this way, Mom."

"What way, honey?"

She bit her lip. "Depressed."

"Because of Rob?"

"Partly. And I don't want to go back to work Monday."

"I thought you liked it in Portland," Myra faltered.

"It's okay. I'm just getting a stark look at the contrast between my actual life and the life I had planned."

"You mean ...?"

"Yes, I mean. The whole nine yards—husband, kids, best-selling novelist."

"You can still write, honey."

Rebecca snorted.

"Seriously," her mother persisted. "Get a notebook and outline your first novel. You can work on it evenings after you go back to work."

"I'll think about it."

"I can't help you with the rest, but I'd really like to see you writing again. You wrote some really cute stories when you were in college."

Rebecca didn't respond to that. Cute stories. It seemed so childish now. If she wrote a book today, it would be full of anguish and desperation. Her journal had been so depressing she'd quit writing in it. The only plots she could think of now would involve broken hearts and anguished souls.

Maybe she could write about the remnants of a fine old New England family living bleakly in a crumbling seaside mansion. In the end, the neurotic parents would die, and the daughter's former fiancé would marry someone normal. Her heroine would jump off the cliff to end her miserable existence.

"I'll see you Sunday, Mom. Keep praying for me."

"I'll never stop."

Chapter 18

Rob drove slowly to the cottage on Saturday, dreading the meeting, even while he longed to see Rebecca again. She'd been so genuinely herself when he'd seen her Thursday, so like the girl he'd fallen deeply, irrevocably in love with, that he hadn't been able to rid himself of the image.

Her surprise when she'd recognized him had touched something deep inside him. Long ago she'd decided she never wanted him to walk into her life again, and he'd broken her wish.

He knew she'd felt neglected and abandoned while he was in California; that much was painfully clear in her messages. He still hoarded the letters and cards she'd mailed him but had long since given up rereading them. Somehow she had decided it was better to end their relationship than to wish in vain it was different, and after all that time apart, his sudden appearance at the cottage had thrown her off balance.

She'd been wearing the same type of thing she'd have worn as a teenager—cutoff jeans, a striped T-shirt, bare feet. Her hair was caught in a thick braid, taffy golden, not the too-pale shade of Brittany's hair. He used to tug Becca's long braid gently when he wanted to kiss her, and she'd always turned toward him eagerly.

And her tears, when she thought he'd left. That had really torn his heart. Leaving after he saw them was doubly painful, and his thoughts had gone back to her time and again over the last forty-eight hours.

She was lounging on the dock this time, with jeans and a long shirt pulled over her swimsuit. An extra chair was waiting.

"Hi." He sat down and appraised her. She seemed calm, ready to talk business, her gray eyes somber. She was more beautiful than ever, and he decided she had reached womanhood while his back was turned. His last glimpse of her, when she saw him off at the airport, had been of a maturing girl.

All right, she'd been twenty-two, but still, compared to the woman who sat beside him now, she'd been a kid. The honey-colored braid was the same, maybe a few inches longer, but her demeanor was definitely different, and it unsettled him.

"Are you all right?" he asked.

"Yes."

"Have you thought about what I asked you?"

She nodded gravely. "I need to know something." She lowered her eyelids and hesitated. "Do you want to buy me out because you want the cottage all to yourself, or because you want to be done with ... with the headaches of dealing with me?"

He thought about that and looked out over the water. The lake was the same color as her eyes today, and not as deep. How many nights had he lain awake thinking about the different expressions those eyes could hold?

"You haven't been hard to deal with," he said at last. "I just thought maybe it was becoming a burden on you, and you'd like an opportunity to make some changes."

"Oh." She looked up at the cottage, and he wondered if it was sometimes hard for her to make the mortgage payments. Her salary must be far less than his, and she paid city rents, while he lived with his parents. But it wasn't exactly true that he was making the offer for her sake.

"I thought maybe—" She glanced at him cautiously, then away.

"Maybe what?" His voice caught a little, and he knew he was losing control. This was why he had dreaded coming. His love for her was there, strong and deep, just below the surface, and if he let her see it, she would have another chance to tell him to stay out of her life.

Why, why hadn't he found a way to take her to California? Married students survived. It was tough, but they did it. And Brazil? If he couldn't take her along, he should have refused that offer. Why was it so obvious now, when at the time he'd felt as if his career depended on accepting it?

Her face flushed, and she looked out over the lake. "I thought maybe you were getting married."

Rob took a ragged breath. "No."

"Because if you were, it would be an awkward situation, like you said."

He thought of Brittany and her fury the night before. Could Rebecca possibly have heard that he was dating a beautiful but ruthless and manipulating woman? How could he have been such a fool?

"No, Bec, I'm not getting married."

She nodded but didn't look at him. He followed her gaze, off toward the island. It didn't matter to him anymore what Eric or Brittany or anyone else thought. They could keep things the way they were. Rebecca loved this place, he could see that now. He didn't want her to feel pressured by his offer, to think he wanted to tear the cottage away from her.

Somehow, the place meant as much to her as it did to him, even if she no longer wanted to share her life with him. How could he have imagined otherwise? He knew her way of thinking, the way she put her heart into everything. It wasn't just the convenience and the restfulness of the place she cherished. They had a history here, and Rebecca was not one to jettison history, even when it was painful.

A speedboat roared past, out beyond the float, and the waves from its wake rocked the float then glided in and slapped the dock. The canoe pulled against the painter, bumping the edge of the dock behind them.

"Hey, you want to go for a canoe ride?" he asked, without much hope.

But she looked at him with a flicker of a smile. "You want to?"

"Sure."

"The other life jacket is up in the shed."

"I'll get it."

He got up and walked to the shed, deliberately slowing his steps to give himself time to calm down. When he got back to the dock, Rebecca was seated in the bow. He handed her the second paddle and tossed his life jacket into the bottom of the canoe, then lowered himself off the edge of the dock and loosed the painter.

By unspoken agreement, they steered for the island. He watched her arms move skillfully. She had always been slender, but she seemed a little too thin now. The breeze caught the tails of her loose chambray shirt, and they flapped a little. Her braid hung glistening down her back, and he wished he could hold it in his hand once more, feel its satiny texture slide through his fingers. She hadn't set out to be enticing, he was certain, but the effect on him as he watched her stubborn, straight back was almost overwhelming.

He steered without thinking about it. All his thoughts were on Rebecca. When the prow touched the sand, she jumped out and waded ashore, pulling the canoe aground. She didn't wait for him, but climbed up the boulders near the shore, hopping from rock to rock. When he caught up with her, she had settled on the biggest boulder and was looking back toward their cottage, tucked beneath the tall pines.

He sat down beside her, unable to keep the raging memories at bay. "Remember when we came here before?"

She nodded, her lips making a thin slash of her mouth. He couldn't read her profile. She might be holding back a smile. On the other hand, she might be near tears again.

They sat in silence for a long time. Her braid hung over her shoulder now, and she looked very young and vulnerable. She shifted a little, stretching out her legs, and her shoulder touched his. Rob reached for her hand and grasped her fingers lightly.

"A lot of water under the bridge," he whispered.

"Would you sell the cottage to someone else?"

"No."

She sat for a minute not speaking, and he dared to stroke her fingers with his thumb, but she took her hand from his and raised her chin. "I've thought about it. Have the papers drawn up, and I'll sign it. Just ... give me whatever you think is fair."

The pain was sharp, and he tried to draw a deep breath. She stood up abruptly and hopped to the next rock before he could speak, teetering as her sneakers grabbed the rough surface. She jumped down to another rock without looking back. Rob rose slowly. She wouldn't paddle off and leave him here on the island, would she? He had no choice but to follow her back to the canoe.

They paddled back in silence, and Rob tried to decide how to approach the subject again. Stronger than ever, he resolved to keep things the way they were, but he'd messed up badly. He never should have listened to Eric. Somehow he had to undo this thing he had set in motion. But he couldn't yell at her the length of the canoe to discuss business. He waited grimly until they landed at the cottage.

"Look, Becca," he said as they walked up from the dock, "we don't have to do this. Let's just leave things alone for a while."

She kept looking straight ahead. "No, you were right. It's time. I have to let go." She paused at the door to the screen porch. "I'm leaving tomorrow morning. I'd like to have the option of coming back next weekend, if you don't mind. Then it's all yours."

"Let's rethink this."

She shook her head. "I've thought about it for two days, and I don't want to think about it anymore."

"Becca, I changed my mind. I don't want to—"

"It's better this way, Rob."

Chapter 19

At three in the morning, Rebecca gave up trying to sleep and got dressed. She walked down to the shore and sat on the edge of the dock, her feet barely sweeping the dark water. It's better this way, she repeated inwardly. He wants to be shed of this whole mess, and it's time.

She couldn't pray at first, but gradually she marshaled her thoughts and formed a plea. *Lord, help me. He wants this part of his life to be over, and I've got to give him that. Please help me to move on, too. I can't cry over Rob forever. You must have something else ahead for me, and I'm ready to accept that. But it's hard.*

She sat until the sun sent its first rays over the tops of the pine trees across the lake, then she went back up the path and began to pack. She changed the bed and smoothed the linens, placing the afghan precisely where Rob had left it. Carefully she inspected each room, to be sure she wasn't leaving behind anything she ever wanted to see again.

She had mentioned to Faye the possibility of the two of them coming up again the last weekend in July. If things worked out, she would bring her. If not, then this was goodbye. She took a few of the books she had brought earlier from the shelves near the fireplace, then paused in the doorway to the bathroom. The red plaid shirt hung there, so innocently. He would never miss it.

No. She turned away resolutely. He wanted to end this. Period.

Her first day back in the ER was exhausting. Faye was out sick, leaving them with an inexperienced receptionist pulled from another floor. The waiting room overflowed with ill and injured people. Rebecca dealt with a psychiatric patient, a stroke victim, and a car thief who had been injured in a scuffle with the police. A patrolman stood poker-faced inside the door to the exam room the entire time his prisoner was being treated, and Rebecca and the doctor walked around him.

Just before her lunch break, Hilda pulled her aside, questioning her charge slips again. Rebecca shuffled through them, baffled. "I don't understand. I'm sure I didn't put four here. That was a one."

"Uh-huh." Hilda didn't sound convinced. She walked away with the paperwork. Rebecca stared after her, a sick feeling billowing in her stomach.

"I'm sure glad you're back," Stacy said when she passed Rebecca with an IV pole, but Rebecca didn't think she really sounded glad. "At least there's somebody else to take the heat now."

"What do you mean?"

"Hilda's been on my back for two weeks. Maybe she'll hound you for a change today."

When at last her shift ended, Rebecca drove home and collapsed on her bed without eating any supper.

Lord, I thought things would get better, but they're worse. What's going on at work? I don't know what to do about this. I can't prove to Hilda that I'm telling the truth. She lay unmoving, letting the tears stream down her cheeks onto the pillowcase. Finally she sat up, blew her nose, and reached for her Bible.

Reading her Bible was the last thing she wanted to do, but she refused to fall into that trap again.

If I quit listening to You now, I'll be worse off than ever, she acknowledged. *So, please, God, help me to stop whining. And if it's not too much trouble, please give me some encouragement tonight.*

She opened the worn leather volume to James 1, knowing what she would find there, but knowing also that she needed it.

"My brethren, count it all joy when ye fall into divers temptations; Knowing this, that the trying of your faith worketh patience. But let patience have her perfect work, that ye may be perfect and entire, wanting nothing."

Trials and temptations. That was the story of her life nowadays. Her faith was definitely being tried, between the trouble at work and Rob's reentry to her life. She hoped she would at least come out of it having learned a little patience. She poured out her heart in prayer, then called Faye.

"Hey, are you all right? I missed you today," she cried when her friend answered the phone.

"I'll be there tomorrow. It was a bad cold."

"I'm sorry."

"How was your vacation?"

"It had its ups and downs."

"Sounds familiar. I was supposed to go to Searsport with Peter Saturday, but I had to cancel. My throat was raw and I was going through a box of tissues a day."

"You really like him, don't you?" Rebecca asked.

"Yes, I do. And if you're interested, he's got a friend who's solvent, sane, and reasonably good looking."

Rebecca laughed. "I don't think I'm ready for that." She hesitated. "Something happened at the cottage."

"What?"

"I saw Rob."

"Really?" Faye's voice rose in excitement.

"Yeah. He came to ask me if I'd sell my share of the cottage to him."

"Wow. What did you tell him?"

"I said I would."

"No."

"Yes. This whole business is driving me nuts, and I figured, if that's the way he wants it, why not?"

"But you might never see him again."

"I might not anyway. You're forgetting, I hadn't seen him in over three years."

"But still—"

"It's a done deal," Rebecca said. "He's going to send me the paperwork. Next weekend is my last chance to use it. Do you want to come with me?"

"I'd really like to, but—"

"Don't tell me. You and Peter have a date."

"Well, yes."

Rebecca drew a deep breath. "It's okay."

The old despair gnawed at the edge of her peace when she hung up. So that was it. She would never visit the cottage again. She went to the dresser and pulled out a nightgown. A cool shower and a good night's sleep, that was what she needed.

The small blue velvet box in the corner of the drawer caught her eye, and she stared at it. *I won't take it out,* she told herself.

She went to the bathroom and took a long shower, then she pulled on the gown and blow-dried her hair meticulously, all the while trying to rein in her emotions. It was no use. Why did Rob have to come around? She padded back to the dresser and opened the drawer. When she snapped open the box, her engagement ring winked up at her.

It was small, as diamonds went. Rob hadn't had much to spend on it. The plain gold setting was of her own choosing. Nothing pretentious, just an outright statement of his undying devotion.

Was it dead now? How could feelings that strong die?

She knew the answer to that. She had killed them. Every time he had tried to set things right, she had beaten him back. Even on the island, when he'd tried to retract his offer. But if she had accepted that and kept her half of the cottage, she would keep these ambivalent feelings for the rest of her life.

The urge to put the ring on was almost overwhelming. She stared at it long and hard, then suddenly snapped the box shut.

Chapter 20

Connie Wallace was surprised when Debbie called her at five o'clock.

"Mom, it's me. Is Dad home?"

"No, dear. He's still at the store." Something in Debbie's voice made her ask, "Is anything wrong?"

"Oh, Mom, it's Mark. He's waiting in the parking lot. His truck is right beside my car."

"Debbie!" Connie caught her breath. "Did you see him?"

"Yes. I was going to lock up, and I went to close the window blind. I saw him out there, leaning on the side of his truck."

"Is Dr. Wilbur still there with you?"

"No, he left a few minutes ago. I'm alone here, Mom. I'm scared."

"Lock the door," Connie said quickly.

"I did."

The front door of the house opened, Rob came in, carrying his leather briefcase.

"Rob's here," Connie said to Debbie. "Hold on a second."

"What's up?" Rob asked, unknotting his necktie. It was hot again, and he had his sport coat over his arm.

"Mark's bothering Debbie again."

"You're kidding." He stepped forward and took the phone from her hand. "Debbie, it's me. What's going on?" He listened intently. "All right, peek out again. Don't let him see you. Is he still there?"

There was a pause.

"Hang up and call 911," Rob commanded. "Whatever you do, don't open the door until the cops get there. I'm on my way. Call them now."

He replaced the receiver and looked at Connie, his face filled with anxiety. "I'm going to go get her."

❧❧

It took him nearly fifteen minutes to get back to Waterville, fighting the summer traffic at the supper hour. When he pulled in at Dr. Wilbur's office, a police car sat in the lot with its blue lights flashing. The office door was wide open, so he walked in.

"Debbie, are you all right?"

She was sitting on one of the chintz-covered settees in the waiting room, and a patrolman was standing in front of her, writing in a small notebook. He looked up sharply at Rob's question.

"He's my brother," Debbie said quickly. "I called him a few minutes ago."

The officer nodded. "All right, Miss Wallace. I think that's all I need. If we can catch up with this Mark Elliott, we'll give him a talking to."

"Can't you arrest him?" Rob asked.

"Well, he didn't really do anything," the officer said.

"But he violated the protective order."

The officer shrugged. "It's Miss Wallace's word against his, unfortunately. The order was issued, what, two months ago? This is the first complaint on it, and he didn't actually *do* anything."

"Isn't there some limit he's not supposed to cross? He can't come this close to her," Rob said, a little belligerently.

"Well, if we can catch him in her vicinity, or, better yet, trying to harass her—"

"It's *better* if he harasses her?" Rob thought he might laugh at the absurdity.

"Well, better for our purposes," the man said sheepishly. "He doesn't live in town, or even in Kennebec County. I can't follow him to Bangor, but we'll ask the Bangor Police to have a word with him."

"Come on, Rob." Debbie got up and reached for her purse. "Thank you for coming so quickly, Officer Trahan."

"You'll see her home?" Trahan asked Rob.

"Yes. And what do we do if he shows up at our house?"

The officer shrugged. He was obviously not happy with the outcome of the incident, but he couldn't offer a good solution. "You live outside the city limits, so you can't call us. The county sheriff's office would handle it." He looked mournfully at Debbie, as if he truly wished he could do more to help her.

They went out together, and Debbie made sure the door was locked.

"If you end up calling the sheriff, be sure and tell them you filed the complaint here today," Trahan said.

"Will that help?" Rob asked doubtfully.

"If they call me, I'll tell them to take it seriously."

"Thanks." Rob looked around as he guided Debbie to her car. "I'll follow you home."

◄○○►

"No, no, no." Debbie sat down on a stool in her mom's kitchen. "I can't hide out for the rest of my life."

"Just for a couple of days, until we know he's not hanging around here," Rob coaxed. "You'll be safer."

"I feel safe here with you and Dad."

"What if he comes around in the daytime, when your mother's here alone?" Stewart asked pointedly.

"That wouldn't be so good," Debbie admitted.

"If he shows his face on our property, I'll call the police," Connie assured her.

"Well, that could happen whether I'm staying here or not," Debbie argued. "I think I'd be more scared at the lake, where there's no phone or anything."

"But Mark has no idea where the cottage is. There's no way he'd find you there, and you could get a good night's sleep," Rob said.

Debbie's chin came up. "He found out where I work now."

That bothered Rob too. "Maybe he waited near here this morning and followed you to work."

"You keep your cell phone handy," Stewart said. "Don't hesitate to call the cops."

"I'll still have to go to work."

Connie placed her hand on Debbie's shoulder. "Mark knows you called the police on him. If he comes to the office, you call the police again. And make sure Dr. Wilbur doesn't leave before you do. Explain the situation to him, and don't go out to your car alone."

Stewart offered, "You can take my car to work tomorrow."

"No, he'd recognize it," Rob said. "I'll take you to work and pick you up after. That will make him wonder, if he drives by the doctor's office looking for your car."

Debbie sighed. "I guess it would be nice to stay at the lake for a couple of days. But I'd be scared by myself."

Rob shrugged. "I could stay there with you, I suppose."

"Might be a good idea," their father said.

Connie looked at Rob. "But isn't it Rebecca's turn to use the cottage this month?"

Rob cleared his throat, embarrassed. "Well, she'll be there this weekend, but she's selling her share to me. After Sunday, the cottage is all mine."

His family stared at him.

"When did this happen?" Stewart asked.

"Last Saturday."

"Well." His father's expression held a hint of pain.

"Yes," Rob said. "But she won't be there for the next few days, anyway. I'm sure she wouldn't mind if I took Debbie down there."

"You should ask her," Connie said.

Rob grimaced. "How about if I give you her phone number and you call her?"

His mother's eyes were the same deep brown as his own, and just as stubborn. "No, Robert, this is something you should do yourself."

Rob glared at her, but she only straightened her shoulders and glared back..

"Call her, Rob," his father growled. "Debbie can go pack her things."

His parents and Debbie left the kitchen, and Rob looked at the telephone balefully. Slowly he walked toward it. He was the last person who should ask a favor of Rebecca. He lifted the receiver and punched the numbers in one at a time. He knew them by heart, although he'd only called her in Portland once.

God, please let the line be busy, if You don't mind.

It started to ring.

She might not be home, he thought hopefully.

After three rings her voice came, wary and a little sleepy. "Hello?"

"Becca."

There was a pause. "Rob?"

"Yes." He stood for a moment, unable to think. His heart was hammering, just from hearing her soft voice in his ear.

"What is it?" she asked a bit breathlessly.

"I—could Debbie stay at the cottage for a couple of nights? Would you mind?"

"Of course not. Tell her it's fine."

"I know you're coming this weekend. We'll be sure she's out of there by Friday, so you can have your solitude."

"Actually, I'd about decided not to come."

"Oh, don't do that."

"Why not?" She sounded surprised that he objected.

Rob squeezed his eyes shut. "I—I just felt when I saw you that you love it there. Don't give up your last weekend."

She was quiet for a moment, then said, "I'll think about it. Tell Debbie to enjoy herself."

"Well, she's not going for fun," Rob said soberly. "We need to get her out of sight for a couple of days."

"What's going on?"

151

"She broke her engagement a few weeks ago, and her boyfriend's been harassing her."

There was a shocked silence.

"She's okay," Rob assured her.

"I'm sorry." Rebecca's voice broke, and Rob thought she was crying. He wished desperately that he could see her, and even more that he could put his arms around her and comfort her. Of course she would be upset at Debbie's trouble. She'd always been that way. He thought again of her empathy after Tommy's death. When people she cared about hurt, Rebecca cried.

Chapter 21

"Brittany giving you the cold shoulder?" Eric asked at the office the next morning.

"What?" Rob looked up from his computer screen, not welcoming the distraction. He'd underestimated the time he needed to get Debbie to work and had come in a few minutes late. Ever since, he'd been trying to regain the lost time.

"I saw Brittany walk past you this morning as if she didn't know you from Adam. What gives?"

Rob shrugged. "I think we're history. Or maybe a tiny footnote in history."

Eric's eyebrows arched. "Well, you lasted longer than most guys."

"That's brutal."

"So's Brittany." Eric clapped him on the shoulder. "Just my opinion, I'd say you're well out of this one."

"You never liked her, did you?"

"I've known her longer than you have, buddy." Eric sat at his own desk, then looked over at Rob. "Do you really like her yourself? You seemed like an odd couple to me."

Rob shrugged. "My first impression of her was that she was a lot of fun. Sweet, too."

Eric grimaced. "Sweet like treacle. Too much of it gives you a bellyache."

"I guess I just ... got into the relationship before I knew her very well."

"Yeah? How long did you know this—Rebecca, is it?"

"Her family lived just down the road. I've known her all my life."

"Sweet?" Eric asked cynically.

Rob's phone rang, and he reached for it, shooting a dark glance at Eric. "Rob Wallace."

"Mr. Wallace, this is Officer Trahan. I came up with some information I thought might interest you and your sister."

"What is it?"

"Mark Elliott's company is working in the area."

"Where?"

"They're building a fast food restaurant in Oakland. I guess they're getting a new burger joint out there."

"Terrific," Rob said with sarcasm. "He's smack dab between Debbie's home in Belgrade and her employer in Waterville."

"I thought of that too. Easy for him to check up on her."

"Why, after all these weeks?" Rob's frustration was showing, and he knew it.

"Well, his foreman told me they've had him up in Houlton for a while, so maybe it was just too far for him to get down here and follow her around until now."

Rob sighed. "I don't know how to keep her safe. The protective order seems useless."

"Your sister seems like a nice lady," Trahan said. "I'd hate to see anything happen to her."

Rob raised his eyebrows. Was Trahan taking a personal interest? Maybe that was a good thing. "She's a terrific girl who got into a lousy relationship."

"Mm. We'll work with the state police on this. Oh, and the construction company's putting the crew up at a motel on Kennedy Drive."

"So he's living within your jurisdiction."

"For the time being," the officer said. "Just keep clear of him if you can. If he turns up again, we know where to find him. Tell your sister to be extra careful if she has to drive through the neighborhood."

154

Rob picked Debbie up at five minutes past five. Dr. Wilbur waved at them as she got into the car, then hurried to his Lexus.

"Everything all right?" Rob asked her as he drove toward home.

"Well, one of the patients said there was a guy hanging around the parking lot after lunch, but when I looked out, I couldn't see him."

Rob scowled. "He's staying at a motel not far from here." He told her what Trahan had revealed to him, and Debbie swallowed hard.

"How long do you think this will go on?"

"I don't know," Rob said. "I can't even figure out why he's doing it." He looked at her quickly. "I mean, I know you're gorgeous, and he was in love with you and all that. I didn't mean to imply there was no reason for him to be cut up after you broke up with him."

"It's okay," she said dully. "I know what you mean. There's heartbreak, and then there's psychosis."

"We'd better be careful when we leave the house for the cottage. I'd hate to have him find out where we're stashing you, kiddo." Rob reached over and squeezed her arm. "It's going to be all right."

She nodded. "I've been praying all day. I don't think I've prayed so much in a year. Funny how we go running back to God when the going gets tough."

"I've been doing some of that myself lately," Rob admitted. "I'm just glad He's always ready to forgive."

Debbie nodded, her eyes glistening. "I've been really stupid this time."

"No."

"Yes."

"No stupider than I've been. Brittany is no better for me than Mark is for you."

She considered that. "At least you recognize it."

On Friday, Hilda Murphy called Rebecca aside. Before she even spoke, Rebecca felt a sick foreboding.

"Rebecca, this overcharging of patients has got to stop."

Rebecca's stomach lurched. "You mean—me? I haven't been overcharging. What would be the point?"

"I don't know what the point is," Hilda said sternly, "but your charge slips are still coming through with too many meds and procedures marked."

"That's impossible."

"Hardly. It happened again yesterday."

Rebecca swallowed her fear and confusion. "Could I see the charts, please? I don't know what you're talking about."

"I've already passed them on to the administrator. I've spoken to you about this before. The board is not happy. Consider this your last warning."

Rebecca stared at Hilda's departing back in disbelief. This couldn't be happening. She'd been scrupulously careful with her paperwork. At noon, she sought Faye out in the break room.

"Why would she believe I'd do something like that?"

"I don't know." Faye took a bite of her sandwich.

"I mean, how could it possibly benefit me to cheat the insurance companies out of a few dollars here and a few dollars there?"

"Well ... if it didn't benefit you, who would it benefit?"

"I have no idea."

"No, come on, think about it," Faye insisted. "Don't you ever read mysteries?"

"Not very often. I try, but I always think I know who did it, then it turns out to be someone else, and it's too frustrating."

Faye smiled. "There were lots of mysteries at the cottage."

"All Rob's."

"I see. Well, one very important thing in a mystery is motive, right?"

"I suppose." Rebecca shrugged in exasperation. "That's just what I was saying. There's no motive."

"Not for you."

"For who, then?"

"Whoever's changing your charts must have a motive."

"Like what?"

"Maybe someone wants to get you fired."

Rebecca stared at her. "Why?"

"I don't know, but it seems as if someone has it in for you. I wonder if Hilda's found discrepancies on other people's charts, or just yours," Faye mused.

"I think Stacy's had some problems. But I don't see how anyone in the ER could have a motive," Rebecca said, lifting her cup.

"How so?"

"The only entity to benefit directly from this scam, if that's what it is, is the hospital."

"You've got a point there. When a nurse overcharges, she never sees the money. It goes to the hospital."

"Right."

"So why do it in the first place?" Faye asked.

Rebecca frowned. "Sometimes I think Stacy does it if she doesn't like the patient."

"What, some perverse way of getting even with grumpy people?"

"I guess that's silly. And we all know about the fuss last year when that story broke on national TV about hospitals charging inconsistently. Everybody's tried to be careful."

"So far as you know," Faye said.

Rebecca stood and gathered her things. "All I know is, I've got to keep a closer watch on my charts."

That evening she found herself heading north, driving mindlessly toward the lake. She couldn't get away from Portland fast enough. When she caught herself letting the needle on the speedometer creep too high, she backed off her speed and hit cruise control.

She pulled into the gravel lot at the cottage and parked beside an unfamiliar car. Uneasily, she grabbed her duffel bag from the back seat and approached the door. It swung open before she reached it, and a dark-haired girl stood facing her, an expectant smile on her face.

"Rebecca!"

"Debbie?" she asked slowly. "Oh, look at you!" Rebecca dropped her bag and rushed to the younger woman, engulfing her in a hug.

"It's so good to see you!" Debbie squealed.

"You, too." Rebecca stepped back and swiped at the tears that came so easily these days. "I didn't expect to find you here."

"I'm just leaving. Rob and I actually moved out this morning, but I left my watch on the sink, and I ran back here to get it."

"You and Rob?"

"Yeah, he and the folks didn't want me staying alone, so he came along as my bodyguard."

"How's it going?" Rebecca asked soberly. "He told me you had some problems with your fiancé."

Debbie grimaced. "Big mistake. I got in over my head with this guy."

"I'm sorry."

"Thanks. The police are watching him—"

"The police?" Rebecca gasped.

"Yeah. He—he hit me a couple of times." Debbie didn't meet her eyes.

Rebecca leaned toward her and hugged her again. "You poor thing. Why don't you stay on this weekend with me? We can catch up."

"No, that's okay. It's your place."

Rebecca smiled ruefully. "Not for long. Did Rob tell you?"

"Yes. Are you sure you want to sell it?"

She shrugged. "It's what Rob wants."

Debbie eyed her carefully. "He said that?"

"It was his idea."

"Since when do you do what he wants?"

Rebecca chuckled ruefully. "Since it got too painful to deal with him. It will be easier for both of us this way." She reached down for her duffel bag and forced herself to think of Debbie's

158

plight, not her own. "Listen, I'd really love it if you stayed. I invited my best friend to come along, but she couldn't, and I was afraid I'd be really maudlin and lonely this weekend. If you were here, we could lie in the sun all day and dive off the float and roast marshmallows."

Debbie was obviously wavering. "Could we play Yahtzee?"

Rebecca laughed. "If there's a Yahtzee game in there, we'll play it."

"There is. Rob and I played last night." Debbie tossed her head, flipping her shoulder-length hair back. "I'll call the folks and tell them I'm staying."

"There's no phone service," Rebecca said.

"Right, but I've found I can text from here on my network." Debbie pulled her cell phone from her pocket. "Dad will be glad. He'll bring my stuff over for sure."

❧

An hour later, while the girls were setting the table for a late supper, Rob knocked at the door.

"I thought Dad was bringing my stuff down," Debbie cried, when she saw her brother bringing in her overnight bag.

"He offered, but I told him I'd do it." Rob's look slid past Debbie and settled on Rebecca.

"Hi," Rebecca said quietly.

"You sure you girls are all set?"

"We're fine," Debbie said. "Why don't you stay and play Yahtzee with us?"

He looked toward Rebecca again, but she was heading onto the screen porch. His smile was a little strained as he told his sister, "That's okay, I've got something to do at home."

Debbie glanced at Rebecca. She had turned her back and was laying out the silverware on the porch table. Debbie looked back at Rob, but his attention was riveted on Rebecca.

"Oh, come on," Debbie coaxed. "It'll be fun. We're just about to eat spaghetti."

"I already ate."

159

"Killjoy."

Rob leaned toward her and said in a low, firm voice, "Give it a rest, Deb. Rebecca doesn't want me here."

"I don't think she'd object."

"Well, you're wrong. She's given no indication whatsoever that she wants to inhabit the same universe with me."

Debbie sighed and stamped her foot impatiently.

"Leave it alone," Rob warned softly.

She made a face at him. "Good night, then."

"Good night." He looked toward the porch doorway and called, "We'll see you, Becca. Call us if you need anything."

"Sure."

He went out without another word. Debbie was a little bit angry with Rebecca. She hadn't even looked at him, although it might be the last time they would ever see each other. Her brother had left with a hopeless disappointment on his face.

Chapter 22

Rebecca allowed Debbie to cajole her into silliness that evening. They stayed up until after midnight, playing games and painting their toenails in ridiculously vibrant colors. On Saturday they canoed for miles, then went back to the cottage and built a fire in the outdoor fireplace. They roasted hot dogs Rebecca had brought and rounded out the meal with potato chips, carrot sticks and canned pudding. A lazy hour on the dock followed, then a swim that somehow degenerated into a splashing contest.

"I haven't had so much fun in ages," Debbie said as she toweled off on the dock.

"Me either." Rebecca laughed. She felt almost carefree.

"It's because there are no men here," Debbie declared.

Rebecca smiled. "There may be something to that theory."

"I'll be meeting the folks for Sunday School and church in the morning. Will you come with me?"

Rebecca sobered. "Oh, I don't know. I've been going to a church in Augusta when I'm here."

"Really? Why? There are so many people at Faith who would love to see you!"

"I just thought it might be awkward."

Debbie stared at her as she wrapped her towel around her sarong-style. "For you or for Rob?"

Rebecca frowned, wondering if she had to respond to that.

"It's because you didn't want to see him, isn't it?" Debbie asked.

"Sort of."

"Well, you've seen him now. No more trauma."

Rebecca chuckled. "If it were only that simple." She wrapped an extra towel around her long hair and squeezed it. "Can I ask you something?"

"Sure," said Debbie.

"Does Rob ... "

"What?"

"Is he dating now?"

Debbie's face wrinkled. "There's this girl, Brittany. I never met her, but Mom and Dad did once. She's totally wrong for him."

"Oh." Something tightened deep in Rebecca's stomach. It wouldn't be so bad if he were dating a nice girl. Immediately she knew she was kidding herself. It would be worse. "So, are they close?"

"I think they had a fight. Rob's talking like he doesn't want to keep seeing her, and personally, I think it's about over."

"But not yet?"

"Well ... He hasn't exactly kept me up to speed. He must see her at work every day. She works in the same office with him. But he told me he knows she's not good for him."

Rebecca gritted her teeth and sat down to put her sneakers on. The wrong woman, but he persisted in dating her. She wanted to ask Debbie to describe Brittany, but she was afraid of her own reaction, so she kept quiet.

"Do you think I should send my ring back?" Debbie asked.

Rebecca stared at her, then looked away.

"Sorry," Debbie said. "I wasn't trying to pry. I only asked because Rob told me he'd told you to keep yours, and I wondered if I ought to send mine back to Mark."

"Did he ask for it?"

"No, he hasn't said anything about it. Not that I want him to get close enough to say anything." Debbie pulled on her sandals.

"It might be easier to get rid of it," Rebecca said. "Then you won't have it there to remind you."

162

Debbie eyed her keenly. "Rob thinks you hate him."

Rebecca felt the throat lump and tears returning. "Debbie, I don't mean to be rude, but I don't think I want to have this conversation."

"I'm sorry." Debbie stood up. "Really sorry. He hurt you a lot, I guess."

Rebecca turned away, toward the lake, but a sob escaped her. She stared toward the island, her back rigid, trying the bring the present back into focus by pushing down the past.

Debbie's hand landed gently on her shoulder.

"I'm so sorry. I shouldn't have brought it up. I figured—well—we've both been through a lot."

Rebecca swallowed. "You were my sister," she choked out.

"I wish I were," Debbie said fiercely.

"Well, don't go blaming Rob for what happened. I was the one who called it off."

"You must have thought it was the right thing to do."

Breathing seemed like a huge chore as Rebecca gulped for air. "It seemed like I waited a long, long time, longer than was reasonable, but now ..."

"I'm confused," Debbie admitted. "I was mad at you for ages, because Rob seemed so crushed, and I love him so much. But now, I can see that you're as shell-shocked as he is. I guess you both took some hits."

Rebecca took a deep, shaky breath. "Yeah. Just give me a few minutes alone, please. I'll be up, and we can play Scrabble."

"Do you want me to go back to my folks'?"

"No, please stay."

"Okay. I'll make tea."

Rebecca heard her sandals on the path, and then the porch door opened and closed. She walked across the dock and sank into a lawn chair, breathing deeply and slowly. Prayer. It was the only thing that could help when she fell apart this badly.

Their Scrabble game ended early. Both girls were yawning by eight thirty. By tacit agreement, they avoided the subject of men. Instead they talked about their jobs, their friends, and books they had read.

"I don't know about you," Debbie said at last, "but I'm exhausted."

"Me too. Let's turn in." Rebecca scooped the letter tiles into the Scrabble box, and Debbie gathered up the empty glasses and popcorn bowls.

When Debbie's light went out in the bunk room, Rebecca lay on the double bed in the other room reading a psalm.

Gradually her emotions calmed. She snapped out the lamp and lay back on the pillows, going over in her mind the many things she was thankful for. The reunion with Debbie, the sister she thought she had lost along with Rob, was an unexpected bonus. She hoped that when she went back to Portland, they could stay in touch. Maybe Debbie would even come visit her in the city one weekend.

The sound of a motor and tires maneuvering the gravel road brought her to attention. A car door slammed. She sat up, her heart racing, and listened. Someone pounded on the cottage door.

She jumped up in the near darkness and fumbled for her robe, then hurried toward the stairs, casting a glance at Debbie's closed door. Had Rob come with a message? The peremptory knock came a second time.

She turned on the kitchen light as the knocking started again, then flung open the door. The man stood frozen in surprise, his fist in midair.

"Who are you?" he asked.

Rebecca shifted uneasily. "Who are *you*?"

He smiled slowly. He wasn't bad looking, with his sun-bleached hair gleaming in the light that fell through the doorway, but his smile made her skin crawl.

"I'm a friend of Debbie's. You must be Rob's ex."

"You're Mark," Rebecca said with certainty. "What do you want?"

164

"Debbie."

"She's not available."

"Her car's out front."

Suddenly Rebecca was afraid. She wished she had woken Debbie and told her to run to the cottage next door.

"Isn't there some law that says you're not allowed to be here?"

He scowled at her. "Debbie has property that belongs to me."

"Oh, really?" Rebecca put all the sarcasm and contempt she could muster into her voice, hoping he wouldn't hear the underlying panic.

Mark reached out and took hold of her upper arm. Rebecca pulled back.

"Don't touch me!"

Too late, she realized her retreat had allowed him enough room to enter the kitchen.

"Leave now," Rebecca said as evenly as she could, her heart thumping.

"I want to see Debbie."

Rebecca considered an outright lie. *She's not here.* No, she couldn't say that. *Lord, I need Your help bigtime!*

"Why don't you call her parents' house and see if you can make an appointment?" she asked, a telltale tremor betraying her.

He smiled again, a slow, canine smile. "Rob sure knows how to pick 'em, doesn't he? And I used to think he was boring." He stepped toward her again, and Rebecca took another step backward.

"Get out," she choked.

His face crumpled in mock sorrow. "Aw. Be nice."

She pulled herself up tall. "In your dreams."

He inched forward. "Hey, come on. I'm a fun kind of guy. What's your name? Rachel? No, that's not it." He came closer, and Rebecca retreated once more, finding her back against the refrigerator. "Ruth? It's something that starts with an R."

"I'm warning you. Get out of here." She tried to say it menacingly, but he reached out and traced the line of her set jaw with his index finger.

"Or what?" His hand settled at the side of her neck, and his fingers toyed with tendrils of her long hair.

Her instinct cried, *Rob, I need you!* But immediately she knew that was futile, and she knew where her real source of power lay.

Lord, I need You!

Rebecca brought her hand up fast and hard, and smacked him with her palm.

He swore, pulling back at the last possible instant, so that the blow connected with less force than she had intended. She dodged quickly to the side, heading for the living room doorway, but Mark grabbed her wrist and jerked her toward him. With a scream, Rebecca stumbled. Rather than fall toward him, she twisted and hit the floor with a heavy thud.

"Mark, let her go!"

They both turned, startled, to see Debbie standing in the doorway. She looked young and innocent in her baseball uniform pajamas, with her dark hair hanging loose about her shoulders. But her eyes were determined, and in her right hand was a thin stick of firewood.

"Hey, Deborah," Mark said with the deceptively charming smile. He straightened and let go of Rebecca's wrist. His breathing was a little rapid, but he acted genuinely pleased, as though he'd unexpectedly run into an old friend at the grocery store.

"You'd better get out of here," Debbie said vehemently. "I've called the police."

Mark's expression changed instantly to rage, and he spat an oath at Debbie that made Rebecca cringe. As the two faced off, she slowly slid away from him and pulled herself up next to the cupboards behind him. Dull pain throbbed through her left shoulder, ribs and hip.

"You'd like to see me in jail, wouldn't you?" Mark asked, his eyes fixed on Debbie.

"If you're going to behave like a thug, yes." Debbie's steely expression gave no quarter.

"I thought you liked things a little on the dangerous side."

"Not anymore. I was very foolish, but I've come to my senses."

"Oh, you're a big girl. You know what you want now."

Debbie hesitated. "I don't want anything you can offer."

"Oh, yeah? How about the two-thousand-dollar ring I gave you?"

"It was twelve hundred, and you can have it back. I don't want it anymore."

He stood for a moment, not breaking the eye contact, and Rebecca realized she was holding her breath.

"You'd better go," Debbie whispered. "The cops are on the way."

"Where's the ring?" he snarled.

"Not here. I'll mail it to you."

"No, I'm not staying in Bangor right now."

"Then tell me where to send it."

"Meet me at the North Street playground in Waterville tomorrow at noon."

Debbie stood still, evaluating him for a moment. "One o'clock, and I'll send my father."

Mark's upper lip twitched. "If I don't get that ring tomorrow—"

"Don't worry, you'll get it. Now go. And I don't ever want to see you again."

Mark's eyes glinted as he held the stare. Rebecca was proud of Debbie for standing her ground, but still afraid Mark would hurt her. She tensed, wildly giving the kitchen a mental inventory for an easily accessible weapon.

Far away, she heard the faint wail of a siren. Mark swore and turned abruptly toward the screen door. He shoved it open, and it swung against the outside wall with a slam. The two girls stared at each other, listening to his footsteps, the car door, and the engine.

When he pulled out of the parking spot and tore up the gravel road, Debbie's rigid posture collapsed. Rebecca hurried across the room and put her arms around her.

"Are you okay?"

"Me?" Debbie asked with a nervous laugh. "You're the one he man-handled. Did he hurt you?"

"I don't think so. You actually called the police?"

"Indirectly. I texted Rob and told him to call them."

The siren was louder, but as they listened, it seemed to retreat again.

"Either they're after him, or they missed the camp road," Rebecca said. "I'm going to lock the door and make us some hot cocoa."

"Put lots of marshmallows in mine."

"You're shaking. Come on, sit down." Rebecca pulled her to a chair. As she turned to close the door, she jumped back with a gasp as headlights flooded the parking area.

"Is it Mark?" Debbie's voice shook. "Shut the door quick."

Rebecca closed the door all but a crack and peered out anxiously, until she recognized the car and its driver.

"It's Rob."

Debbie got up and pushed past her, rushing out into the darkness, and threw herself into her brother's arms.

"You should have called 911," Rob scolded gently as he brought her back inside.

"You know I can't from here. Anyway, you called them, didn't you?" Debbie asked.

"Yes, but we'd better get a landline put in here. If you'd called them first, they might have gotten here before he took off."

"Are they chasing him?"

"I think so. Just before I got to the road, a dark pickup went flying past me, with a squad car right behind it."

Rob kept going into the living room and pulled Debbie down onto the sofa with him. He had on worn jeans and a soft blue plaid shirt. His jaw was dark with a day's whiskers, which for some reason sent a stab of longing through Rebecca. He could grow a beard in two weeks, she thought in amazement. He'd tried once, the summer after high school graduation, and given it up after a month, disgusted with the sparse, silky growth. He wouldn't have a problem now. She swallowed, trying to adjust her mental concept of Rob as mature.

"Are you girls okay?"

Debbie nodded, and Rebecca said quietly, "We're fine, but it was a near thing."

Rob gently pried Debbie's fingers away from the stick of firewood. "Did you use this on him?"

Debbie giggled a bit hysterically.

"You need a fire." Rob went to kneel at the hearth. He pulled some small sticks and bark from the woodbox and deftly arranged the kindling in the fireplace.

"I was going to make some cocoa," Rebecca said softly.

"Sounds good." He didn't look up.

She turned toward the kitchen.

Chapter 23

"Rob, he wants the ring back," Debbie said.

"So give it to him."

"I will. But I left it at Dad's. He told me to take it to him tomorrow at that playground in Waterville."

"North Street?"

"Yes. One o'clock."

"I'll go."

"All right. I told him Dad would come."

"No, let me do it," Rob insisted. "If he's not in jail, that is." He didn't want his father to go one-on-one with Mark. He struck a match and watched with satisfaction as his tinder caught. "You sure you're not hurt?"

"He didn't touch me, but..."

"But what?" Rob snapped.

"Don't bite me."

"Sorry." He ran a hand through his hair, trying to calm his runaway nerves. "I was worried about you."

"Well, he was bothering Becca when I came downstairs."

"What do you mean, bothering?"

"He—he had hold of her arm, and I think he was—well, he intimidated her for sure. I don't know what he said before I came in. And he—he sort of threw her on the floor."

Rob scowled as a new level of anger coursed through him. "Why don't you go get your bathrobe?"

"You forgot to bring it," Debbie said.

"Here, take this." He eased the afghan off the back of the sofa and wrapped it around her. "Sit tight."

Rebecca was stirring a pan of cocoa at the stove. He walked over to stand behind her, and she gasped, turning quickly.

"Sorry," Rob said. "I didn't mean to scare you."

She smiled sheepishly. "Not your fault."

"Look, the cops will probably come back here after they either get Mark or lose him. They'll want to question you and Debbie."

She nodded. "All right. I guess we can handle that."

"Not alone. I'll stay until we hear from them. In fact, I'm thinking I'll go call Dad and tell him I'm sleeping on the couch here tonight."

"Oh, no, that's not necessary." She looked up at him, then turned hastily back to her pot of cocoa.

Rob stood for a moment, trying to settle his frayed nerves. She looked so endearingly silly in her red plaid bathrobe and bare feet, with purple toenails peeping out from beneath the hem, and her honey gold hair streaming free down to her hips.

"Becca, I'm staying. Period."

She turned halfway around again, with the wooden spoon in her hand. "All right, Rob."

He smiled slowly. She wasn't insisting that he leave this time. That was progress. "Thank you."

He wanted very much to put his arms around her and offer her the same comfort he'd given Debbie. As their eyes locked, something seemed to soften there for an instant, but then she retreated, holding herself a little stiffer, maintaining an independent, self-sufficient aloofness.

His heart ached. He didn't want Becca to become someone who didn't welcome comfort, but he couldn't force his tenderness on her. She still chose to hold him off. Nothing had changed there, although she and Debbie seemed to have picked up their friendship where it left off.

"I'd like to get dressed before the police come," she said.

He nodded. "Sure. I'll take over here." She put the spoon in the pan and stepped away from him, as if to avoid any chance that he might touch her accidentally.

"Becca," he said, angry that his throat felt constricted with anxiety, "Debbie said Mark was bothering you."

Rebecca sighed. "I didn't know she was awake, and I wanted to keep him from knowing she was here, but he guessed anyway, because of her car. Rob, how did he know about this place? Debbie said it was a secret."

"Not really a secret, but I didn't think he knew where it was." He shrugged, remembering how Brittany had ferreted out the information she wanted. "I guess anyone could find out with a little digging. I'm sorry this happened. I thought she'd be safe here, and I let my guard down."

"Don't blame yourself." Rebecca drew in her breath, as if she would say more, but the words evaporated as she looked him full in the eyes.

"I shouldn't have let you two stay here alone," he said. "Are you hurt?"

"Not seriously."

He reached toward her. "You're sure?"

"Yes. I'll be fine."

He looked deep into her gray eyes and decided she wasn't downplaying her injuries. She was a nurse. She would know if she needed medical attention. "All right. Be sure and tell the police everything."

She nodded.

"Becca, about the cottage," he said softly, pleadingly.

"Let's not go through that again. If you want to change something, just write it up the way you want it. I mean it. Whatever you want, Rob, but don't be overly generous."

He winced. She didn't even want to hear his case for calling off the deal. She'd always been like that; once she made up her mind, there was no changing it. It had been an asset, when she was his steady girl, then his fiancée. He'd thought Becca would never back out of that promise, and he'd felt secure in her love. It was the only time he could remember her changing her mind

173

like that. It was so out of character, it still jarred him to his toes every time he thought about it. He cleared his throat. "I'll be fair."

"That's all I ask."

She went quickly, and he watched her hair bounce and float a little as she walked through the doorway. He heard her murmuring tones as she spoke to Debbie, then the stairs creaked.

When the cocoa was ready, Rob turned off the burner. Debbie had dozed off on the sofa, and he sipped a mug alone, watching her sleep and wishing Rebecca would come back down. She was avoiding him, that was obvious. She didn't want to talk to him anymore, or look at him, or give him a chance to talk about the cottage or the past.

She stayed in her room a long time, but he could hear her moving about above him. She came down when the patrol car arrived, dressed in jeans and a sweatshirt, with her hair braided and the purple toenails hidden in sneakers. She brought her own robe and handed it to Debbie.

When the state trooper talked to her, Debbie was tearful again, and her account of the incident meandered. Rob sat beside her, plying her with tissues. When the officer questioned Rebecca, she was quiet, direct, and coherent.

"We've got him in custody," the trooper said. "But he'll probably make bail tomorrow. Did he hurt you physically, Miss Harding?"

"Not really. At least—" Rebecca pushed back her sleeve and examined her forearm. "I think I'm all right. I may have some bruising from the fall."

"Do you need pictures?" Rob asked.

"No, I don't think that's necessary," the officer said, "but you may need to testify on the assault charge if this goes to trial."

When he had ushered the trooper out, Rebecca met Rob in the doorway between the kitchen and living room.

"I changed the bed upstairs," she said. "You can sleep up there."

"No, I'll be fine on the couch."

"Rob, it's your room. It's your cottage now."

He frowned at her. "Forget it. I'm sleeping on the couch."

He saw a glitter in her gray eyes, and he thought at first she was angry, but then she sniffed a little, and he decided it was tears he glimpsed. He seized the moment, reaching for her, cupping her face in both hands.

"You're not going to win this one, Becca," he whispered. "I get the couch."

She nodded slowly.

He smiled then. "Want some of that cocoa now?"

"No, thanks. I'll get you some blankets. And thank you, Rob. For everything."

Chapter 24

She lay awake for hours, tossing restlessly, but trying not to let the bed creak when she rolled over. At last she lay curled on her side, facing the window. She could see one black rectangle of sky, spattered with tree limbs and sprinkled with tiny, glinting stars. She ought to have told Rob she'd changed her mind and didn't want to sell, after all. He'd given her leeway for that.

Thoughts of the woman who was all wrong for him weren't helping her insomnia. Debbie had said Rob wasn't completely happy in the relationship, but he was still seeing the blonde. Brittany.

The image of the woman who had come looking for Richard Smith three weeks ago came unbidden to her mind. Had Brittany come to check up on Rob? To see what his ex-girlfriend looked like? Was it possible, or was she being paranoid?

She had resisted the urge to pump Debbie for more information about Brittany. Debbie would pounce on it and accuse her of jealousy and coax her to admit she still loved Rob madly. And she wouldn't be able to deny it. Best to forget about the woman in the fancy car. It didn't matter, really, who she was.

Unable to sleep, she turned once more to prayer and felt some relief. She prayed for each member of the Wallace family, her own parents, her sister, and Faye. She sought the Lord's guidance in her situation at work, and she ended her lengthy prayer with a petition for Mark Elliott. She wasn't sure how to pray for him. She knew she could forgive him, but she would never trust him, and she hoped she never had to face him again.

By dawn she was calmer, but there was still one thing unsettled in her heart. Even if Rob despised her for the way she had treated him, she needed to ask his forgiveness. She couldn't maintain a close walk with God and go on resenting the way Rob had left her all those years ago. She needed to let go of the hurt at the same time she let go of the cottage, and then maybe she could truly let go of Rob Wallace.

All right, Lord. If You'll go with me, I'll go down and talk to him. I'm no good to You if I carry bitterness around, and I want this to end.

She rose quietly and dressed in the graying darkness, then tiptoed out into the hall. If he was asleep, she would wake him up. But first, she couldn't help thinking, she would watch him sleep for a minute. It had been so very long since she'd had the opportunity to watch him, the right to look at him as long as she wanted to.

As she descended quietly into the living room, the sound of an engine catching outside the cottage made her freeze, then hurry on down. Her heart stilled. The sofa was empty, the blankets neatly folded and stacked with the pillow on top. And Rob was gone.

❧❧❧

It was all she could do not to back out on Debbie that morning. When she hinted she might head back to Portland early, Debbie began to cry.

"Becca, you can't. We're going to Sunday school. Please. You promised. You can't leave now."

Remorse swept over her when she saw how emotionally fragile Debbie was. If it hadn't been for the scene with Mark last night, Debbie would have been more resilient, she was sure. But right now she was vulnerable. Her brother had skipped out before daylight, and she needed her friend's support.

178

They ate an odd breakfast, cleaning up the leftovers in preparation for Rebecca's departure from the cottage.

"Will Rob move right back in here?" Rebecca asked, frowning as she looked at the quart of milk, half head of lettuce, and dish of spaghetti still in the refrigerator.

"I don't know. You can leave that stuff. If he's not going to come right away, I'll clean it out."

They drove to church in Rebecca's car, and she found herself swept up in a flurry of hugs and welcomes. The pastor and his wife embraced her, begging her to eat dinner with them, but she declined. When the Wallaces came in a minute before the Sunday School hour, Connie went straight to Rebecca, her arms wide.

"Dear girl," she breathed in Rebecca's ear. "Thank you for standing up for Debbie. You've got to come to the house today."

"Thank you, but I don't think I can. I need to head out after the service."

Stewart pulled her into a bear hug. "We've missed you, little lady."

Rebecca brushed away a tear. "I've missed all of you too."

"Could have fooled me," Stewart chided.

She colored a little. "I'm sorry. It just seemed—better—somehow—not to—" She let it trail off, and Connie squeezed her arm.

"There, now. Don't let Dad Wallace upset you. He's been pining for you a little, is all."

Rebecca managed a shaky smile. How long could she hold up under the onslaught of their love? She wanted to ask where Rob was, but she didn't dare. That would open the flood gates, for sure.

As if she'd picked up her thoughts, Connie said confidentially, "Rob's going to be a little late. His friend Eric called him this morning, needing some help with his car. Rob didn't want to go, but he can't say no to people who need help."

"It's a good thing he came home early this morning," Stewart said. "If he hadn't, I might have had to go help Eric."

Rebecca sat rigidly between Connie and Debbie, but gradually began to relax as the Sunday School lesson progressed. This was her home church, and these people were her spiritual family.

Her family had moved three years ago, but she still knew eighty percent of the parishioners, and they seemed glad to see her. A good number of them came over to greet her after Sunday School, and Rebecca found herself basking in the warmth of their love. The church she had visited couldn't come close to this, and the bigger church she'd found in Portland still felt impersonal, but this—this was home.

The worship service began, and she tried to keep her mind off the fact that Rob had yet to put in an appearance. He came in about ten minutes late and dropped softly onto the end of the pew, beyond Connie and Stewart, without looking at her.

Rebecca caught her breath and stared at the pastor. Her one quick look had told her Rob was impeccably groomed. He was wearing a dark gray suit and pearl gray shirt, with a brighter necktie that spelled sophistication. He looked like the respected architect he was, and she didn't feel quite comfortable with this side of him yet. She hadn't grown into the world of business and success with him, the way they had planned.

When the ushers took the offering, she risked another quick glance and found he was solemnly eyeing her. She looked away quickly, but not before she had noticed, with some comfort, that his cowlick still showed a latent tendency to rebel. The old Rob was still there.

"You'll come for lunch," Connie said as soon as church was done.

"Well, I—" She looked helplessly at Debbie.

"Come," Debbie insisted.

She glanced at Rob, and he was watching her, but there was no smile there. She looked away. "I ought to go."

"I'll get Deb's ring and head out to Waterville," Rob said.

"Do you know if Mark made bail?" Stewart asked.

"I called the police station just before I came, and they let him go last night."

"Last night?" Connie's voice was shrill with anxiety. "I thought they'd at least keep him until Monday."

Rob shrugged. "The county jail's overflowing."

Fear shrouded Debbie's face. "Do you think he'll leave me alone when he has the ring back?"

"I hope so," Rob said noncommittally.

"I'd better get going," Rebecca said.

"Oh, please stay." Connie touched her arm, and Rebecca hesitated.

"I—I think I'd better go. I'll have to be at work early tomorrow and—I'd just better go."

She held her purse and Bible close to her and walked swiftly to the entry, shook hands with Pastor Fields, and went out into the baking sun. As she took out her car keys, Rob came and stood beside her, leaning his elbow on the roof of her car.

"Rob." The keys fell to the pavement, and she stooped, blushing, to pick them up.

"You don't have to run off because of me."

"I—I'm not. I just—" she shrugged, her heart racing. The suit was definitely a great look for him.

"If you want to visit with the folks, I can stay away for a while. They'd love to have you."

She fought back tears. He was offering to keep away from his own home for her sake. Was it because he didn't want to be near her, or because he thought she didn't want to be near him? She shook her head vigorously. "Don't do that. I should really get back. And you—you ought to move right back to the lake. If you want to. It's yours now."

"It's still July."

"Only for a couple of days, and anyway, I'll be gone. This is it for me. Send me the papers, won't you?"

He grimaced. "Are you sure?"

Now was her chance. She stood very still, wondering if she dared. Could she go on alternating time at the cottage with him, now that she'd seen him again, especially since she'd renewed her contact with his family?

His family. They'd be a huge drawing card for any woman. Who could help loving the Wallaces?

And things had gotten much more intimate this summer. The canoe, the shirt, his night on the sofa, even if it had been for Debbie's sake. Could she ever come back to the cottage and find peace again? Her heart was in upheaval now.

"This is too hard," she whispered.

He stepped back a little. "All right, Becca. If that's the way you want it."

He walked across the parking lot, and she stared after him.

Chapter 25

Rob pulled into the parking lot and looked over the busy playground, his heart thudding. Mothers were sitting on benches watching their children swing and climb on the equipment. It was busy and noisy. He didn't like the idea of meeting a potentially violent man here, but he supposed it was better than a deserted spot. He'd prayed during the short drive for wisdom and a speedy end to the meeting, and his parents and Debbie were praying at home.

In his peripheral vision he saw a man rise from the bench at one of the covered picnic tables, and he immediately faced him and zeroed in on Mark. Rob walked slowly toward him, looking around as he went, gauging the distance between the picnic table and his car, and between Mark and the nearest bystanders.

Mark stood waiting, and Rob stepped in below the low roof, onto the concrete pad that held the picnic tables.

"Where's Debbie?" Mark asked.

"You didn't expect her to come, did you?"

They took each other's measure. Mark's hair and eyebrows were bleached almost white by the sun, and his face and arms were deeply tanned. His blue eyes held a watchful, feral look. "I didn't do anything to her."

Rob took a deep breath to calm the almost overpowering impulse to hit him. Once for Debbie, and again for Rebecca. It would feel good. For a moment, anyway. And then some hysterical mother near the swings would rightfully call the police on her cell phone, and Rob would be carted off and booked for assault. Mark would ice his jaw and laugh.

"I know exactly what you did," Rob said. "I suggest you stay away from my folks' place and mine. And don't go near Debbie's workplace again."

Mark's jaw worked back and forth a little, as though he was debating whether or not to address that. "You threatening me?"

"No." Rob shook his head. "I'm just stating a fact. If you bother Debbie or anyone connected to my family again, you'll regret it."

Mark chuckled mirthlessly. "You think you're something, don't you? Protecting all the women around you. Well, I could take you down in two seconds flat. You wouldn't know what hit you."

"Maybe so." Rob stood firm, knowing most bullies were full of talk, but also remembering Mark's record for acting on his rage. He glanced toward the playground again. One of the mothers seemed to be watching while she buckled her toddler into a stroller, and he felt marginally safer.

Maybe Mark could beat him up, maybe not. Rob was taller, but their weight was about the same. No doubt Mark had a lot more experience street fighting, and his rugged build was proof of the physical labor he performed daily. At least Rob was reasonably sure he wouldn't dare pull a weapon in front of witnesses and risk being hustled to jail for breaking parole.

Suddenly Mark smiled. "I liked that gal at the cottage. What's her name? Ruby? No, that's not right. Rachel? I don't know how you manage to attract these classy women, but you seem to have trouble hanging on to them. Maybe I could give you a few lessons."

Rob gritted his teeth. "I'm serious. You keep away, or you won't bail out so quickly."

"Oh, calm down. You don't want to get hurt now, do you?" Mark spit on the ground outside the picnic shelter. "Where's the ring?"

Rob reached into his pocket, brought out the small box, and extended it. Mark looked at it for a moment, then quickly seized it and opened the cover. He squinted at the diamond, then snapped the case shut and slipped it into his own pocket.

He glared at Rob. "You tell Debbie I'm glad I found out how disloyal she is, before we tied the knot."

"I'll tell her no such thing."

Mark stepped toward him, his fists clenched. Rob braced himself and was glad he'd changed out of his dress clothes.

Suddenly Mark's attention was caught by something behind him, and Rob fought the urge to turn and look. Maybe Mark was just trying to distract him. But his opponent's expression changed from wrath to disgust.

"Oh, you weren't man enough to come alone, huh?"

Rob turned around then and saw a city patrol car nosing into a parking spot beside Mark's pickup. As he watched, Officer Trahan got out of the car and ambled toward them.

"I didn't ask for backup," Rob said in a low voice.

"Right. Of course you didn't." Mark shoved past him, his hands in his pockets, and walked straight toward Trahan.

"How's it going?" the policeman asked when Mark was ten feet from him.

"Leave me alone. I'm not breaking any laws."

"Just be sure you don't," Trahan said. "As long as you're in this town, we're watching you."

Mark swore and made a beeline for his truck. Trahan looked after him as he peeled out of the parking lot and headed toward the downtown. When Mark's pickup was out of sight, he turned to Rob, shaking his head.

"Second time he's cussed at me today."

"You tailing him?" Rob asked, joining Trahan on the grass near the squad car.

"Not exactly. Just letting him know we're here. Too much of that and we'd be harassing him. But we're doing a thorough check on him, since the county sheriff arrested him in Belgrade the other night."

Rob nodded. "Well, thanks. You might have just saved me a trip to the emergency room."

Trahan shrugged. "Just doing my duty. Of course, when a citizen calls and tells us where a felon on bail is scheduled to be, we get curious and want to make sure he doesn't stir up any more trouble."

"A citizen called you?" Rob asked. "My dad?"

"Nope." Trahan looked at him, then looked around the parking lot and the playground. "Your sister."

"Debbie called you?"

"Well, she called the station, and they paged me. She was worried, I guess. Said you were handing over some valuable property to this Elliott, and she wanted to make sure the transaction went smoothly."

"It did."

The patrolman nodded, still not looking at him. "Glad to hear it. I told her I was sure you were capable of taking care of yourself, but since I had time I'd just cruise by here. We'll keep an eye on him. Gotta be careful with hot-tempered fellows like that."

◁◯▷

Rebecca managed to get away from the hospital at noon on Tuesday, and she and Faye went out to lunch together. The restaurant was crowded, but the air conditioning felt sublime after the stifling heat outside. Rebecca ordered a chicken salad, and Faye sat opposite her with a cheeseburger.

"You always make me feel guilty," Faye complained.

"Whatever for?"

"You're eating skinny food again and drinking a diet soda."

Rebecca smiled. "I make a pig out of myself at the cottage. That's the only place I let myself eat junk food anymore."

"You're disgusting."

"I had to make some sort of rule. My eating was getting out of control last spring."

"But you won't be going to the cottage anymore," Faye pointed out. "Are you giving up milkshakes forever?"

"Guess I'll have to come up with a new system. How about if I only eat junk food with you? No, that won't work. We eat lunch together every time we can."

Faye laughed. "How about, only one day a week?"

"Hm, I could eat a lot of ice cream in a day."

"Tell me about it." Faye said ruefully.

"So, what's the big secret you were going to tell me?" Rebecca asked.

"You'll never guess."

"Okay, so tell me."

Faye looked disappointed. "I guess I might as well, because you really could never guess."

Rebecca sighed. "All right, I'll try."

Faye grinned.

"Does it have something to do with Peter?"

Faye's jaw dropped. "How did you pull that out?"

"Oh, I don't know. Best friend, big secret, hunky boyfriend."

Faye giggled. "It's not like that."

"Good. I was afraid you were going to tell me he proposed, and it's way too early."

"Good grief, yes."

Rebecca scowled, thinking. "So, it has to do with Peter, but marriage is not at issue."

"Right."

"Hmm ... does it have to do with your date this weekend?"

"That's no secret. We're going to Old Orchard Beach."

"Okay, let's see. You told me he's going to law school at night. I know! He passed the bar exam."

"Not yet. He's got at least another year. But it has to do with his job at the restaurant."

"Someone left him a lottery ticket for a tip, and he won the jackpot."

Faye threw back her head in a howl of laughter, then looked around self-consciously. "I'd better just tell you."

"Yes, I think I've entertained you long enough."

Faye leaned toward her conspiratorially. "He overheard something in the restaurant."

Rebecca widened her eyes in an exaggerated look of inquiry. "And that would be ...?"

"Three of the hospital's board members were eating together, and they were talking about the financial side of things."

"And Peter found this to be interesting?"

"Very. It seems the hospital is in a very precarious state right now."

"How precarious?"

"Peter thinks it's really bad. He was serving them, and they all just kept talking like he wasn't even there. You know, like he was the butler or something."

Rebecca nodded.

"One of them was Mr. Tanner."

"The chairman of the board?" Rebecca asked.

"I'm sure of it. Peter described him to a T, right down to his pot belly and his pocket watch."

"So?"

"So, these three board members were bemoaning the hospital's poor cash flow. You know they poured a lot into that new cancer unit last year."

"I thought some rich guy donated the money for that."

"There was an astronomical overrun on the budget when they built it."

"Really?"

"And that's not all. Some foundation that was bankrolling the Pedi ICU went belly up." Faye looked around again and lowered her voice even more. "They said that if Pouchard doesn't turn things around by the end of the year, he's out."

Rebecca sipped her drink while she thought that over. "If the administrator can't make the hospital profitable again, they'll fire him?"

Faye nodded significantly.

"Well, that is interesting, but I don't see what it has to do with me."

"Come on, you're smart. Put it together."

"What?"

"All this overcharging business."

Rebecca stared at her. "You're nuts. How could Mr. Pouchard have anything to do with that? The chief administrator doesn't come into the ER and add charges to patients' charts."

"Somebody's doing it. Supplies, procedures, but mostly drugs. That's the hospital's biggest profit maker. Patients get charged for doses they never got, or they're charged twice for what they did get. And the hospital rakes in a few hundred extra dollars."

Rebecca didn't want to believe it was a systematic practice, but Faye's arguments were sounding more and more credible.

Faye sat back and popped a french fry into her mouth. "Listen, while you were gone, I did some investigating. I didn't want to say anything until I had something solid, but with what Peter heard, it's all starting to make sense."

"Whoa," Rebecca cried. "You and Peter are playing detective?"

Faye shrugged. "Sort of. And I found out that while you were on vacation, the overcharges didn't stop."

"I know I'm not the only one."

"No. It's happened to Lindsay, Kelly, Mike, Sandra, and Stacy. Stacy's the worst."

"I thought she was doing it herself," Rebecca mused.

"Maybe once in a while, but she was crying about it last week. It's become epidemic."

"Is Hilda harassing everyone about it?"

"I heard her get after Stacy, but other than that ... And I have no idea whether or not it's happening on other shifts, you understand. That's just on the day shift."

Rebecca nodded. "Very interesting. Stacy did say something to me on Monday. But what can I do?"

Faye shrugged. "I tried to find a pattern, to see if it only happened when a certain person was charge nurse, but that doesn't seem to be the case."

"Well, the one in charge would certainly be in the best position to change charts."

"Right. But it happened when at least three different nurses had their turn. Including Stacy, I might add."

"So, she could be behind it, or she could be an innocent victim, like me."

"Could go either way," Faye agreed.

Rebecca took a deep breath and exhaled slowly. "It makes no sense."

"I agree. I figure there's a pattern, but I just wasn't bright enough to work it out."

"Don't sell yourself short. You made more progress than I made in months of puzzling over it."

"So you agree that what Peter heard in the restaurant is connected to this?"

"No," Rebecca said slowly, "I wouldn't go that far. I'd say it's possible, though." She smiled at her friend. "You and Peter make a pretty good sleuthing team. Are you sure he wants to be a lawyer? Maybe you should start a detective agency."

Faye's smile was dazzling. "And to think, when I first met him I thought he was just a waiter."

Chapter 26

Officer Ned Trahan rode up the elevator at Hanson Associates, observing the firm's offices with interest. Pretty classy. The receptionist downstairs had fresh flowers on her desk. The furniture was heavy and solid, like classics in a museum. Carpet a mile thick deadened his footsteps, and the plaster detail on the ceilings said *Money!*

He knocked softly on the door he'd been directed to.

"Come in!"

He opened it and peered inside. Rob Wallace was sitting at a drawing board, and another young man was hunched over a blueprint spread on a big walnut desk.

Rob jumped up. "Officer Trahan. This is my friend and coworker, Eric Plourde." Eric eyed his uniform and nodded cordially but with an inquisitive air.

"I came to give you an update on your sister's case," Trahan said to Rob.

Eric stood up quickly. "Hey, excuse me, I'll give you a few minutes. You want some coffee?"

"No thanks," said Trahan, and Rob shook his head.

"What's happening?" Rob asked, when he had seated the patrolman.

"Mark Elliott. As you know, we've been watching him, and he's still staying at that motel with his work crew."

Rob nodded. "No one in my family has seen him."

"No, he seems to be toeing the line right now."

"Good. That's a relief."

"Well, like I say, we've been watching him."

"I do appreciate that. When Debbie filed for the protective order, it seemed like nobody cared."

"We got some reports on him from other law enforcement agencies." Trahan watched Rob closely, and he nodded. "Found out he had a record."

"Here?"

"No, but up in Bangor he had an assault rap, and he was arrested once in Farmington for OUI, when he was on a construction job down there."

"That doesn't make me feel any better. I wish he was in jail."

"It's not likely, unless he acts up again," Trahan admitted. "He'll probably get a suspended sentence for bothering your sister and her friend. Might serve a few days."

"That's it?"

Trahan shrugged. "We don't do the sentencing. It's up to the judge."

"But if he's been arrested for assault before—"

"That might help. So, anyway, like I say, we've been keeping an eye on him, but the sergeant says we can't keep it up forever. Not enough manpower. But Elliott took an interesting ride on his lunch hour today. I thought you'd want to know."

"What?" Rob tensed. "Did he go to Dr. Wilbur's office again?"

"No. He came here. I followed him."

"Here?" Rob stared at him, startled. "Whatever for?"

"Well, I wondered that myself. Thought maybe he was here to make trouble for you. I was all set to follow him in, but he didn't come inside."

"No?"

"Nope. Sat in his truck in your parking lot until a blonde came out."

"He met someone?"

"Yup. Having lunch with a woman who works here. She's a real knockout. Late twenties, five-foot-six, drives an RX7. You know her?"

192

Rob's jaw dropped. He tapped his silver pen on the edge of his desk several times, then looked Ned Trahan in the eye. "I know her."

❧❧❧

At quarter to four, Rob stretched and appraised the drawing he had finished. It was good, and the hospital board would love his concept of their new pediatrics wing.

"I'll be back in a sec," he said to the back of Eric's head.

"Mmm." When Eric was immersed in a project, he was in another world. They had that in common, and Rob thought that was part of what made them work so well together. They left each other alone for long stretches of time, and neither one took offense.

Rob rode the elevator to the ground floor and strolled into Brittany's office, his hands in his pockets.

"Hey, Brit, I hear you've been seeing someone new."

She looked up at him with icicles in her eyes. "As if you care. Don't tell me you're jealous."

"Not a bit. But I know Mark Elliott."

She quickly veiled a flash of surprise. "Yes, he told me he was a friend of yours."

"We're not friends."

"What are you, then?"

"He used to go with my sister, Debbie. She broke up with him because he was abusive."

Brittany bent her head over the papers on her desk, but he could tell she wasn't working. "How do you mean that?"

Rob grimaced, weighing the consequences of telling Brittany something he'd rather not make public. "He hit her."

She pursed her lips for a moment. "Scout's honor? Because with me he's always been ... well I can't say a gentleman," she laughed, "but he's never been violent."

"It's the truth. Debbie has a restraining order on him, and she's filed complaints with the police. They arrested him Saturday night for violating the protective order."

"Oh, come on! I saw him today."

"He's out on bail. Brit, I'm serious. Be careful."

"I'll take it under advisement," Brittany said breezily, standing up. "I'm a big girl, Rob." She brushed past him in the narrow doorway, trailing one hand across his chest as she passed.

"Meaning?" he called after her.

"If you're just jealous, get over it. If you're truly concerned about me, thank you. I can handle Mark."

Chapter 27

August was nearly over. Portland sizzled, and Rebecca dreaded leaving the air conditioned medical center each evening for her sweltering apartment. She hoarded her paychecks, wondering if she could afford an a.c. unit and still have enough to pay the bills.

She picked up her mail as she let herself in on the twenty-seventh, and tossed it on the table with her purse, then opened the kitchen window and turned to the refrigerator for a cold drink. When she turned around, she saw a manila postcard peeking out from under the electric bill, and she picked it up.

Rebecca, If you want to use the cottage in September, it's all right. I'm making a few changes. Hope you don't mind. RW

She mulled that over. She hadn't heard a word from Rob for the past four weeks. Now he was offering her the use of the cottage one last time, and he was "making changes." To the cottage, or in his lifestyle?

She had expected him to send her a copy of the contract, but August had flown by, and she hadn't heard from him. It was his month to pay the mortgage, but the property tax was due, and if he hadn't changed the deed yet, it was her obligation to pay it.

She popped the tab on her diet cola. Rob should be paying all the taxes now, anyway. Maybe he was busy and had forgotten, the way he'd forgotten to write to her from California.

She hated herself for thinking that, and she breathed a prayer of confession. *Lord, it's over. We both know it. Help me to get rid of the bitterness too.*

She felt a little better. Maybe she ought to run up there Labor Day weekend and ask him what was going on. Thrash this thing out for once and for all, get the paperwork finished, and be done with it.

❧❧❧

"I'm sorry, Rebecca, but I have no choice," Hilda said to her on Friday, but Rebecca couldn't find a trace of remorse in her voice. "I've been told to cut two positions in this department, and considering the irregularities in your paperwork—"

"Hilda, please," Rebecca protested. "I didn't do it. And I really need this job."

Hilda frowned. "You're a good nurse. I don't understand this compulsion."

"What compulsion? I told you, it's not me doing it!"

The department head sighed. "If you could just give me some evidence ... I just can't keep you on."

Rebecca blinked back tears. "Could I go on the night shift? I'll work 11 to 7, I don't care."

"I'm sorry. My decision is final. This will be your last shift here."

Rebecca's shoulders drooped as she went to the reception area. A patient was just finishing being registered and leaving the cubicle.

Rebecca leaned over Faye's desk. "Can you take a break?"

Faye looked up. "I think so. I'll get Lisa to cover for me."

"Meet me out in the ambulance bay."

Faye's eyes were wide, but she nodded. Rebecca went out quickly and stood leaning against the concrete wall. It was cooler today. Summer was winding down, and she felt as if she had missed most of it. The weight of Hilda's announcement was crushing her, and she made herself take deep, ragged breaths so she wouldn't break into sobs. The door opened and her friend came out.

"Faye! I'm being canned. Downsized."

"What? That's crazy. We're always shorthanded."

"Can't help it. I asked if I could go on the night shift or something, but it seems I'm way down the seniority list, and Hilda still thinks I'm overcharging."

"I'm so sorry! I hoped we could get to the bottom of that. What will you do?" Faye's green eyes were woeful.

"I haven't had time to think about it. Go to my folks, I guess. Maybe I can get on at the hospital down there." Rebecca sighed. "I really don't want to do that."

"How about going up to the cottage for a while?" Faye asked. "It's a good place to sort things out."

"No, I told you, Rob's going to buy me out."

"That was ages ago. Has he sent you the money?"

"Well, no, but he will. I hope. September's my month to pay the mortgage, and the property taxes are due the first."

"If he's buying your share, he should pay all that now," Faye contended.

"But he hasn't bought it yet, so it's still my responsibility."

"Call him and remind him. He must make piles of money."

Rebecca stood thinking about that for a long time after Faye left her. The postcard had come. She had his permission. Technically, she was still half owner, and he'd invited her to use the cottage for another month if she wanted to. Why not take him up on it? A mixture of anticipation and gloom assailed her. She prayed silently as she went back to her duties.

On her lunch break, she called her landlord and arranged to give up her apartment immediately. She called information for the phone number for Hanson Associates, Rob's employers, but she couldn't make herself call him. How could he have been sincere in saying she could go to the cottage, when he'd told her he wanted it exclusively in his name? No entanglements, no headaches.

That night she wrote the check for the taxes on the cottage. It nearly wiped out the balance in her checkbook. Again her fingers hovered over the telephone buttons. She turned away and began to pack.

When her clothes, dishes, books, and the two house plants were boxed up, it was after ten o'clock. She pulled her stash of cleaning supplies from under the bathroom sink. The fumes from the cleaning solution made her eyes water as she mixed it into a bucket of warm water. The next two hours were a frenzy of scrubbing. The apartment had to be clean enough so that she'd get the cleaning deposit back. It had to be.

Chapter 28

A blue pickup truck sat in the parking area at the cottage, and its bed was piled with four-by-eight-foot sheets of wallboard. The front door wasn't locked, and Rebecca stepped inside cautiously. Staccato pounding came from overhead.

She walked slowly through the living room, noting that the rough bookshelves had been removed from the far wall, and the books and games were in boxes, stacked on the floor. A sheet of clear plastic covered the sofa and coffee table, and a fine white dust lay over all the surfaces. Between the studs all around the room were the foil sides of Fiberglas insulation batting. She mounted the stairs and peered into the bedroom from which the noise emanated.

"Mr. Wallace!"

Stewart jumped and turned around.

"Rebecca!" He smiled broadly. "Rob didn't think you were coming, so we decided to get started. We've got things pretty well to pieces here."

She stepped into the room. The bed had been dismantled, and the mattress and box spring leaned against one wall, covered by a sheet. More insulation lined the walls, and Stewart was mounting the wallboard over it.

"What's going on?"

"Winterizing."

"Rob plans to spend the winter here?"

"Yup. He got permission from the town planning board. The septic system is good, and they didn't have a problem with him making improvements to the place."

"That's ... terrific," she said uncertainly. "So, you're insulating."

"That's all done. Now we're covering it up. Rob went down to the store to fetch more screws and some staples for the staple gun." Stewart put his left hand against one of the studs and leaned on it. "We had to fix the ceiling."

Rebecca looked up. "Sure enough." Where the underside of the roof had been exposed, there was now a sheet rock ceiling.

"We put twelve inches of batting in the attic, and six in the walls," Stewart said with a touch of pride. "You'll be nice and snug."

She nodded. "Great. I guess – well, I guess I'd better find another place to stay."

"No, Rob won't want that. I'm sure we can finish up this room today, if you want to just ... well, maybe you could go visit with Connie. She'd love to see you. We'll get the wall board on in here. Rob can tape it and finish it when you're gone."

Rebecca swallowed. "Could I help?"

"Certainly! Here, put a mask on. Don't want you breathing Fiberglas." He removed a paper mask from a package for her, and Rebecca pulled it on.

When Rob came in half an hour later, she was helping Stewart measure a piece of wallboard that would fit around the bedroom window.

"Hey, Dad, who's your helper?" Rob called from the doorway. He grinned at Rebecca. "Sorry. If I'd known for sure you were coming this weekend, I'd have held off on this mess."

She pulled off her mask. "It's okay; I should have called, but I didn't really make up my mind until the last minute. You had no way of knowing."

"How about a coffee break?" Stewart asked.

"Sure, Dad."

Stewart laid down his tools and headed for the stairs. Rob lingered, watching Rebecca. She knew she was covered with sheetrock dust, but his eyes held the tender look that melted her inside.

"I—I need to talk to you," she said, looking down at the tape measure in her hand.

"What about?"

"I was hoping I could stay here a few weeks, but—" She looked up at him and saw concern and maybe something more. "Rob, I lost my job."

"Oh, hey, I'm sorry." He stepped toward her but stopped just short of touching range. "Of course you can stay here. Is there anything else I can do?"

She shrugged. "You haven't sent me the papers." His blank look discomfited her. "You know, for the buyout."

"Oh." He nodded slowly. "Do you need some cash?"

"Well, I—" She hesitated, not wanting to admit how close to broke she was. "Were you going to pay me soon? September is my month to make the payment."

"Forget that," he said. "I'll pay from now on. You didn't pay the taxes, did you?"

"Well, yeah. It was due today."

"I'm sorry, Bec. I sort of lost track, I guess. I'll pay you back."

"You don't need to."

"Do you have money for now? Groceries and stuff?"

"Well, I'm a little low," she admitted.

He pulled out his wallet. "Here. Here's a hundred. The bank will be closed Monday for the holiday, but I'll get you a check Tuesday. I promise."

She took the money with a grimace. "Thanks. I just—well, if you want me to leave, I can go to my parents', I guess. I don't want to be in the way here."

"No, stay. Please. That would be too far for you to drive today, anyway, when you just came up from Portland."

She bit her lip. "Are you sure? You weren't expecting me, and I don't want you to have to change your plans."

"I'm positive. Let's go talk things over with Dad. We can make you comfortable in this room by tonight, I think, and Dad

201

will keep working on the other rooms during the week, if you can stand the commotion. Or, hey!" His eyes brightened. "I've still got some vacation left. Maybe I can wangle getting next week off, and we can get it all done and be out of your hair for the rest of the month."

"You're going to live here," she said, and wished she hadn't. It had come out wistfully, and Rob seemed ill at ease.

"Do you mind?"

"No. I just didn't expect it."

"I hadn't thought it out last time I saw you, but once I got the idea, I knew it was what I wanted."

She nodded.

"Come on," he said. "I smell coffee."

◙◖◗◙

At noon, Connie Wallace arrived with a hot casserole.

"Rebecca! It's so good to see you!" She pulled Rebecca into her arms joyfully.

Rob stood watching. This was how it should be. "Becca's going to stay here for a few weeks, Mom."

"In this mess?" Connie held Rebecca at arm's length. "You'd better come to the house until they're at least done with the wall board."

"Oh, no, I couldn't." Rebecca glanced self-consciously toward him, and Rob knew she was still ill at ease around him.

"Well, then, I'd better stay and help you this afternoon," Connie said.

Rebecca took plates from the cupboard and went to set the table on the screened porch. She stopped in her tracks in the doorway, then slowly set the plates down.

"Rob?"

"What?" He went and stood close behind her.

"There's glass in the windows."

"Thermal windows, so we can heat this part, too. But they open for screens. Do you want me to open them now?"

She shook her head.

202

"Are you okay? You're not upset, are you, Bec?" The last thing he wanted to do was change the cottage into something she wouldn't recognize, wouldn't love anymore.

"No. It's wonderful."

He said softly, "I was thinking you might want to sit out here when it's cooler. It gets chilly nights, in September. I know you've never complained, but—"

"Rob!" She whirled and crashed against him, and he put out his hands to steady her, then let them slide around her, pulling her gently against him. "Rob," she choked, "I won't ever be here again after this month. You know that."

"Shh." He threw a glance over his shoulder. Stewart was filling water glasses, and Connie was taking the foil covering from the casserole. "Let's eat now, and we'll sit down later and talk, all right?"

She gulped and nodded, dashing tears from her cheek with the back of her hand.

Rob closed his left hand around her glossy braid and tugged it lightly. She pulled away from him, but she was smiling through her tears. He smiled back before he turned and went into the kitchen. "Glasses ready to go in?"

"Yup." Stewart was refilling the ice tray. Softly, he asked, "Son, are you going to court that girl again?"

Rob stopped with his hands on the cold, wet glasses. "I don't know, Dad. Part of me says I'd be crazy to try."

"Ha!" Stewart shook his head. "You'd be crazy not to."

Rob winced. "She doesn't want me, Dad. She just now made it clear, she's out of here for good the end of September."

He carried two of the tumblers to the porch. Rebecca stood with her back to him, looking down toward the lake. Was his father being wildly optimistic? He had a deep conviction that the hope fluttering in the back of his brain was unreasonable, and he wasn't sure he could survive the agony of her rejection again.

Chapter 29

They stayed on the job all day. It was past seven that evening when they put the bed back together, and Connie helped Rebecca put on the sheets.

"I think this room, at least, is dust free," Connie said with a weary sigh.

"Thank you for all you've done," Rebecca told her. "You'd better go home and get some rest, so you won't be sleeping in church tomorrow."

Connie smoothed the wrinkles from the bedspread. "You shouldn't have to work for your lodgings."

"I don't mind. It's actually been fun today, working with you all. I think I needed to do something strenuous."

Stewart and Rob were straightening up the tools when they went downstairs. "You sure you'll be okay alone tonight?" Stewart asked. "Debbie's gone for the weekend. Otherwise she could stay with you."

"I'll be fine."

"I'm going to have a phone put in for you first thing," Rob assured her.

"After what happened with Mark, I won't feel easy until I know you have one," Stewart agreed.

When they were gone, Rebecca locked the door and went straight to bed. Her last conscious thought was, *He said it's for me.* Of course, she knew the telephone would be for his own use in the long run, but it still felt good to know Stewart and Connie and Rob all cared about her.

On Sunday morning, she woke to a gray drizzle, but it couldn't dampen her feeling of anticipation as she got ready for church. No more vacillating on where she would worship. She brought in two boxes of clothing from the trunk of her car and rifled them, looking for a suitable outfit. She had no idea where her iron had ended up. At last she settled on a dress that shed wrinkles easily.

When she entered the little church, Sunday School was beginning. She searched the pews quickly. Rob was sitting with his parents. Rebecca hesitated, then slipped into an empty spot beside Elsie Fields. Her old friend grinned at her in silent greeting.

After the worship service, Connie Wallace approached her. "Rebecca, dear, you'll eat with us today, won't you? Debbie should be home soon."

"I'm sorry," Rebecca said. "I've told Elsie I'll eat at the parsonage today. Maybe—maybe next time."

Connie nodded. "I'll keep after you. Stewart and Rob want to get some more done on the sheetrock this afternoon, if that's all right with you."

"I don't mind. I know they want to get it done as quickly as they can."

Rebecca enjoyed her visit with the Fields family, but while she was at the parsonage, her thoughts kept straying to the cottage. When she drove back to the lake that afternoon, Debbie greeted her at the door with a huge hug. She was wearing jeans and a ragged sweatshirt, and a fine dust dulled her hair.

"I'm so glad you came back to us, Rebecca! I'm not glad you lost your job, but you're not one to cry over spilt lemonade."

"I think you're mixing metaphors," Rob said. He was holding up a piece of drywall while his father applied the screws.

"The Lord works in mysterious ways," Stewart said, between the whirrs of the power screwdriver.

Rebecca laughed and brushed away the dust Debbie had transferred to her dress. "I'm going to put on some work clothes and join you." As she hurried up the stairs, she realized she felt a renewed joy, even though she had no idea what lay in her future.

By evening they had finished installing the sheetrock in the downstairs rooms, and on Labor Day they taped the seams and applied joint compound. Debbie had the day off from work, and she and Connie came along to help once more, bringing an overflowing picnic basket.

Rebecca continued consciously to let go of her stress and enjoy being part of the family again. She even found that she could banter with Rob about the remodeling project without breaking down in tears.

"I'm sorry we made such a mess here," Connie said as she cleared tools, work gloves, and rolls of tape off the porch table at lunch time.

"Don't apologize. I'm the one who crashed the party," Rebecca laughed. She knew all the work was for Rob's sake, but the Wallaces acted as if they were invading her home.

"Rob could have waited to do this," Debbie said as she distributed paper plates around the table.

"Think of all the fun we'd have missed," Connie replied.

"And it would be too cold to do all this later," Rebecca said. "I'm glad he went ahead with it. He'll be comfortable here this winter."

"I'll be the only tenant at the Wallace B & B when he moves out." Debbie sighed.

"Yeah, well, you'd better behave yourself or you'll be evicted," Rob called from the kitchen.

∞∞∞

Stewart came alone Tuesday morning.

"Rob's gone to the office this morning, but he's hoping to get the rest of the week off."

Rebecca nodded and began to help him unload more supplies from the truck. Debbie had also gone to work, and Connie was occupied at home, so it was just the two of them

207

that day. Working with Stewart would be a pleasure in itself, Rebecca knew, but her arms and shoulders already ached as they carried the materials in.

He winked at her as he handed her a new package of sandpaper. "A little more training and I can hire you at the hardware store."

"Now that's an idea."

He laughed. "You won't have any trouble getting another nursing job, but if you need a reference, put me down."

"Thanks. Who's running the store today?"

"I've got some capable employees down there."

Rebecca nodded. "How's Debbie doing with the new job?"

"Fine. She's wasting her talents at that doctor's office, but I haven't said so. It's kind of nice having her home again. Oh, here. I almost forgot." He handed her a paper bag.

"What's this?"

Stewart shrugged. "Something Rob said you might use."

Rebecca opened it and peeked inside. Four composition books, and a box of a dozen ball-point pens. She smiled and set it on the mantle.

"I'm going to make a lot of dust today," Stewart warned, putting a new roll of paper in the sanding block. "You'd better run in to town or take a long canoe ride."

"No, I'll help you," she insisted.

"Don't want you breathing a lot of sheet rock dust."

"What about you?"

"I'm old."

She laughed. "You're not over fifty."

"Ha. You're wrong, missy."

"Fifty-one?"

"Fifty and a half."

"Oh, that's ancient. But age has nothing to do with this. I'll wear the mask, and we'll get it done in half the time."

He grinned. "Maybe I'd better hire you. Can't afford nurses' wages, though. Can you fix a lawnmower?"

"Not unless an IV will do it."

At noon they both got in the pickup, and Stewart drove to his house. Connie greeted them on the porch, appalled at their appearance.

"I'll get the broom. You two dust off out here. You look like snowmen."

"My dandruff's getting a little thick," Stewart muttered, swatting at the front of his shirt.

"You'd better get a shower here, Rebecca," Connie suggested.

"We're going right back as soon as we eat," she protested. "I'll wait until we're done for the day."

"Well, Rob had better appreciate what you two are doing for him."

When they drove back to the cottage, a dark green sedan with an antenna mounted on the trunk was in the parking lot, and a man stood at the head of the lake path, looking down toward the water.

"Cop," Stewart grunted.

"How can you tell?" Rebecca asked, scrutinizing the car and the man's nondescript suit.

"It's an unmarked unit. See the blue lights in the back window? And that high-powered antenna is a dead giveaway."

Stewart opened his door and got out, walking toward the man. Rebecca got out, too, but stayed near the truck.

It was warm, and the man had shed his jacket and loosened the knot of his necktie. As he spoke to Stewart, glancing occasionally toward her, Rebecca waited and wondered what had brought him out to the lake. She sent up a wordless prayer, not knowing what to ask for, but aware that she was afraid. Maybe Mark was acting out again, and the police were warning the Wallaces.

Stewart and the man came toward her.

"Miss Harding?" the stranger asked. He was nearly Stewart's age, his dark hair sprinkled with gray.

"Yes."

"This is Detective Keyes," Stewart said. "From Portland."

Rebecca gulped.

209

"I'm investigating some irregularities at the hospital where you worked until Friday."

Rebecca felt light-headed. She reached out and grabbed the edge of the pickup bed, afraid she would collapse. Had the hospital administration filed a complaint against her?

"Are you going to arrest me?" she whispered.

"No, ma'am."

She tried to say thank you, but it wouldn't come out. She felt herself swaying and clung to the side of the truck.

"Here, honey," Stewart cried, jumping to her side. "Let's go inside. You need to sit down."

Rebecca clutched his arm and tried to focus on him. "They think I did something wrong," she said. How could she ever explain it, when she didn't know what had happened?

Stewart put his arm around her. "It's all right, we'll straighten it out. Are you okay? Can you walk?"

She nodded miserably and went with him toward the cottage, not looking at the detective, embarrassed that she had to lean on Stewart.

He took her through the chaos of the kitchen and brushed the dust from one of the porch chairs with a rag. "Sit. I'll get you something." He left Detective Keyes to fend for himself and went to the refrigerator, returning with a pitcher of iced tea and three paper cups.

"Here, darlin'. You need some sugar." He poured a cup for her and put it in her hand, then served Keyes and himself.

When she had sipped the tea, Rebecca felt a little better, and she sat up straighter and faced the detective. Stewart sat between them, at the end of the table, and she was grateful for his rational, solid presence. It was almost like having her own father there.

"Can you answer a few questions now, Miss Harding?" Keyes asked.

"Y-yes. I think so. But I really don't know much."

He took a small notebook from his pocket. "It was brought to our attention several months ago that the Ainsley Hospital was making some hefty drug charges to its patients' insurance companies. Two companies complained, and we started an investigation. It took some time, but the data emerged showing that a lot of the charges were indeed superfluous, and that most of them originated in the emergency room. Were you aware of this?"

Rebecca swallowed. "I was accused of padding my charge slips, but I didn't do it. Some of the other nurses had the same problem. Honestly, I didn't do anything like that. On days when I was in charge, I tried to check all the other nurses' slips carefully. It got so that I didn't dare put my charts down. I was afraid someone would change them while I wasn't looking."

Keyes nodded. "And you had no idea who was behind this?"

"The department head—Hilda Murphy—"

Again he nodded.

"She seemed to think it was all my doing, but Stacy Roberge got in trouble, too. I don't know about anyone else for sure, but—but I know others had overcharges." Rebecca looked pleadingly at Stewart. "Dad Wallace, you've got to believe me. I didn't do it."

Stewart squeezed her hand. "Of course not. Why would you?"

"Exactly. My friend Faye and I—she's a receptionist in the ER—we tried to figure out the motive."

Keyes was flipping the pages in his notebook. "Faye Roman?"

"Yes, sir."

"I interviewed her. She's the one who told me how to find you."

"Then she told you all this."

"Yes, and more besides." Keyes cracked a smile for the first time. "I told her she ought to go to the Criminal Justice Academy."

"Then you know about Peter and the restaurant and their detective work."

"Yes, she told me quite a tale."

"Do you think it adds up?" Rebecca asked.

"They were onto something, all right," Keyes admitted. "She begged me to solve this case and clear her friend's name."

Stewart shook his head. "I guess you'll have to bring me up to speed later, Rebecca. I had no idea you were going through such a rough time."

She turned to him, earnest in her desire to keep his respect and love. "They fired me because of this. My supervisor wouldn't listen to me when I told her I had nothing to do with it. She kept giving me warnings, and I tried to be extra careful, but last week she just called me over and told me I was done."

"She needed a scapegoat," Keyes said.

"What? Hilda was doing it? Then why didn't she just keep quiet? Why make such a fuss about it and blame me?"

"Because of the investigation. When people started asking questions, she needed someone to blame, to draw attention away from herself."

"But ... this has been going on for a long time."

"The investigation began in April. I expect she was doing it long before that, but you nurses never knew it because she changed your records after you turned them in to her. You never suspected her?"

Rebecca frowned. "It occurred to me once, but she was the one finding the errors, so I figured she couldn't be doing it. Why would she point it out, if she was responsible?"

"She'd been at it for at least six months before the complaints were filed. We had to move slowly to lay the groundwork and keep from spooking anyone, but it seems Pouchard and Murphy found out about our investigation. After that, they started looking for someone to blame."

"Pouchard? He's the administrator."

"That's right. His job was on the line. No offense, but he had a lot more to lose than you did, miss. He was pulling down a big salary."

"The board told him they'd let him go if he couldn't put the hospital back in the black," Rebecca said slowly. "That's what Peter heard in the restaurant, anyway."

"Yes, so Pouchard and Hilda Murphy cooked up this overcharging scheme. When the charge nurses gave her the charts each day, she would just add a few extras—a dose of narcotic here, an X-ray there."

"I don't understand why Hilda would do that. Was she that altruistic, wanting to save the hospital?"

"Not the hospital. Pouchard."

"Oh." Rebecca felt a bit ill as she absorbed that. "Oh!"

"Precisely. Mrs. Pouchard is very bitter."

"Well," Stewart said softly, "what does all this mean to Rebecca? You didn't drive all the way up here from Portland to shoot the breeze."

"I wanted to hear Miss Harding's side of it. I'd say you were wrongfully terminated. You and Stacy Roberge probably have grounds for a civil suit if it comes to that. But I wouldn't be surprised if you get an offer from Ainsley Hospital soon."

"Stacy was fired too?" Rebecca gasped. "I didn't know that."

"Yes, when Murphy learned of the investigation, she quickly began to lay the blame on her nurses. It seems Roberge had made a few errors previously, so she was an easy mark. Murphy had been told to downsize her department anyway, so she picked you and Stacy Roberge and made it look like you were the troublemakers. Of course, she'd have to quit overcharging when you two left. She milked it for all it was worth, though."

"More than it was worth, by the sound of it," Stewart said, sipping his iced tea.

"You may need to testify in court later, Miss Harding." Keyes drained his cup.

"But you understand I didn't really *know* anything. I just guessed."

"The court will want to hear what happened to you. You know your paperwork was tampered with, and Murphy gave you the gate. It's a small part of the evidence. If you can document any of the incidents it would be helpful. Did you keep a journal, for instance?"

"No, but I did tell Faye about some of the things that happened. I remember one of the first times when I realized it was serious was the Monday before Memorial Day, because I asked Faye to come up here with me that weekend, and we talked about it."

Keyes made a note. "Good. She might remember that occasion. Do you remember anything else specific?"

"Not really."

"Well, if you do, I suggest you write it down."

Rebecca nodded. "When will it come to court?"

"Oh, not for several months, I imagine. The district attorney will notify you. I need your current address."

Rebecca smiled bleakly. "I don't exactly have one."

Stewart raised his chin. "You can reach her in care of me." He gave Keyes his home address and telephone number and walked the detective to the door. Keyes thanked them again and drove toward the main road.

"You all right, darlin'?" Stewart asked, returning to lean in the porch doorway.

"I'm great, thanks to you. Sorry I was so wimpy at first."

He shrugged. "I had no idea what you were dealing with. You should have told us the whole story when you came up here the other day. Don't you know friends can lighten a load like that?"

"You have," she said fervently. "You've all been so great."

"Been praying for you," Stewart said gruffly. "Come on, apprentice. Time to get this job back on track."

Chapter 30

Rob hurried down the block from the lawyer's office, back to Hanson Associates. His lunch hour was only half over, and there was a phone call he wanted to make. He entered the lobby and took the elevator to the second floor. When the door opened, Brittany was waiting to enter.

"Brit?" He stared at the sling that supported her left arm.

"Don't say a word." She shoved past him to enter the elevator.

Rob got off but turned around and held the door open. "What happened?"

"Let go of the door, Rob." She turned her frosty eyes away from him. He thought her face was paler than usual, and through a wash of foundation there was a hint of a bruise on her left cheek.

"Brit, tell me this has nothing to do with Mark."

Her chin came up a notch. "It has nothing to do with *you*. Now let go of the door."

He let it go, and it slid shut, blocking her from his view. He walked swiftly to his office and rummaged in his desk drawer for Ned Trahan's business card. The police station's dispatcher forwarded his call to Officer Trahan in the duty room.

"Oh, hello, Mr. Wallace. I was going to go by Dr. Wilbur's this afternoon and see your sister."

"Where is Mark Elliott?" Rob demanded.

"In the county jail."

"Is he going to bail out again?"

"No, they arraigned him this morning, and I think he's staying a while. The judge set the bail pretty high. We had the evidence we needed this time. Severe injury, and a couple of witnesses."

"When is his hearing?"

"Soon. They don't drag their feet on cases like this. Should be within a week or two. He's probably looking at a year in jail."

"If the sentence isn't suspended."

"It's his second arrest in six weeks. I think he'll do some time. We can hope."

Rob felt calmer as he reminded himself that the district court judge was not the ultimate authority. "I'll do better than hope. I'll pray about it. Thank you."

"Don't you want to know the details?" Trahan asked.

"I think I saw the details in the elevator here a couple of minutes ago."

"Oh, yeah. I forgot she works with you. I'm surprised she made it to the office today. She was in a lot of pain Sunday night, when I saw her at the hospital."

"I tried to warn her about him, when you told me you'd seen them together."

"Well, you have no cause to feel guilty. They'd both had a few drinks that night, and she claims he got rough when she refused to let him stay over at her place. He denies it, but her neighbor was just coming home, fortunately for Miss Dexter. He might have done worse to her if it hadn't been for that."

Rob sighed. "Thanks for telling me. Will you keep us posted? Debbie needs to know if he's released."

"He hasn't come 'round her again, has he?"

"No, but I'm not sure she'll ever stop looking over her shoulder. Rebecca Harding, too."

"Do you think Miss Wallace would mind if I dropped by her office and gave her the news this afternoon?" There was a shy quality to Trahan's voice that made Rob smile.

"I think it would be a big relief to her, to hear it straight from you."

He hung up still smiling, then sobered as he flipped through his address book. *Lord, it's up to You now.* He took a deep breath and punched in the ten digits.

"Mr. Harding? It's Rob Wallace."

"Rob? Hey! Call me Ed. How are you doing?"

"Fine, sir. I need to ask you something."

"What is it, son?"

Rob cleared his throat. "How would you feel about me ... reentering your daughter's life, sir?"

There was a moment's pause, and Rob's adrenaline surged.

"Scratch what I said a second ago," Ed said heartily. "Call me Dad."

◆◆◆

"We'd better run to the store and get some paint this evening," Stewart said as he sanded the wallboard in the spare room. "What color do you want in your room?"

Rebecca laughed. "It's only my room for a couple more weeks, Dad. You'd better ask Rob what he wants."

Stewart looked a bit crestfallen. "You sure you won't stay?"

She pulled her mask down so that it dangled from the elastic around her neck. "How could I? You know this is all for Rob. It was his idea to winterize it. He's probably been wanting to live here year round for ages, but didn't dare to ask me if I'd sell. Well, he asked and I did, so that's that. He can pick the colors."

"Still, you always had good taste," Stewart said. "I'm sure Rob would go along with anything you chose."

She smiled at him. "Are you trying to upset me?"

"No, no. Of course not. Is that what I'm doing?"

"Not quite."

"I'm sorry."

She pulled her mask up over her face and wielded her sandpaper briskly.

They worked agreeably together without talking much, but Rebecca thought Stewart watched her a bit anxiously. Finally he called a coffee break, and she gladly went downstairs with him to open the bag of muffins Connie had sent along with them.

"Look, I didn't mean to make you feel uncomfortable earlier," he said as he sat down. "Connie and I are so happy you've come back. I don't like to hear you talking about leaving again. And I don't mind telling you, we've been praying something would happen."

"What kind of thing?" Rebecca asked, but she thought she knew.

"I guess it's no secret. We've been hoping you and Rob would patch things up."

She buttered her blueberry muffin slowly and deliberately before she looked at him again. "Listen, Dad Wallace, I love you all, your whole family, and I appreciate your concern. I really do. But I don't think Rob had me in mind when he decided to do all this remodeling."

Stewart looked at her sharply, then shrugged. "I don't know everything that's passed between you two. Maybe there's something big that I don't know about."

It was almost a question, and Rebecca bit her lip. "We've hardly had any contact for going on four years."

"I know, but ..." Stewart took a bite of his muffin and chewed thoughtfully. "The way I see it, what's past is in the past. Either you've forgiven him, or you haven't."

Shame brought a flush to Rebecca's cheeks. Stewart was assuming his son was to blame in their break-up, but she knew now that a major part of the guilt was hers.

"Are you still angry with him?" Stewart asked softly. When she didn't answer, he picked up his glass and took a sip. "None of my business, actually."

"I'm not angry," Rebecca said at last. She owed Stewart that much, at least. "I assumed he had other interests by now." She got up and went to the refrigerator for ice cubes, aware that her face was scarlet.

"Hmm. Well, I don't suppose it's up to me to put you straight on that. I think you and Rob need to sit down and talk. That's right," he said as she looked at him in surprise. "You two need to get away from all this pounding and sawdust and nosy parents. Get off where it's quiet and you can thrash this thing out."

She swallowed, but she didn't know what to say. She sat down again and plopped two ice cubes into her drink.

"I'll tell you one thing," Stewart went on. "The happiest day of my life was when Rob told me a few weeks ago he'd got things right with the Lord. But he's the one who needs to tell you the changes he's made since then, and I'm talking about his life, not this house."

"I don't know if he'll talk to me about things like that," she whispered.

"Do you want him to?"

She nodded, unable to trust her voice.

"Well, like I said, you two need some time and opportunity to discuss things, and I don't mean wallpaper."

☚☞☜

Stewart left at supper time, and Rebecca pulled the tarp off the sofa and sank onto the lumpy cushions exhausted, every muscle aching. Thanks to Stewart, she had perfected the art of sanding joint compound smoothly. Tomorrow he would initiate her into the painter's guild, he'd said. That was if he and Rob settled on the paint colors tonight, and if she could move in the morning.

She thought about fixing herself some supper. Stewart had invited her to eat at the house, but she had truthfully pleaded fatigue. There were leftovers in the refrigerator. She closed her eyes. A little nap, then maybe she'd get up and fix a bite.

She woke suddenly to a crackling noise and sat bolt upright.

Rob was crouched before the fireplace, feeding a small blaze with kindling.

"Sorry. I didn't want to wake you up, but it's getting cold in here."

"Thanks." She felt a little befuddled. "What time is it?"

"Seven thirty. I'd say my dad's been working you too hard."

219

She stretched, wincing at the pain that screeched through her back and arms.

Rob hefted two logs onto the fire, then dusted his hands and came to sit beside her. She shifted a little, so her shoulder wasn't touching his, and yawned. "Excuse me. Hey, thanks for the notebooks."

He smiled. "I thought maybe, if the carpenters get out of your way, this would be a good time for you to start putting your research on paper."

She couldn't help smiling. "That's a nice thought. But I have a date with a paint roller tomorrow."

"Oh, no. You have a date with me."

"I do?"

"Yes."

"Didn't you get the paint tonight? Because I really don't think I should be the one to pick it out. I told your father."

"We got it. But Dad and the pastor will be painting. You and I are taking the canoe to the island. If you want to. I mean—well, I'd like it if you did. Please?"

The yearning in his voice made her heart lurch. "And let them do all that work alone?"

"Mom and Dad insisted. They think we need some time to talk without being interrupted. Please?"

She looked at him for a long time, but she couldn't discern what was going on behind those huge brown eyes. He had a desperate earnestness, and she couldn't ignore that. She wondered how much Stewart had told him. At last she said, "Okay. Did you bring the papers for me to sign?"

A look of chagrin crossed his face. "No. I forgot and left them at home. You want me to go get them?"

"You don't have to. Bring them with you tomorrow."

"You want to go to the bank in the morning? I'll get you a cashier's check to pay you for your share."

"No hurry. Did your dad tell you about the visitor we had this afternoon?"

"Yes." His face tightened. "Why didn't you tell me, sweetheart?"

She found it hard to breathe steadily. "I—I didn't think we were on that level."

He eyed her longingly. "I want to be. I want you to tell me things."

"Well, you know it all now." She made herself look away from his face and watched the flames leap and take hold of the maple logs. His nearness was warming her quicker than the fire was.

"I wish I'd been there for you when you were having such a tough time," Rob said softly. "Sounds like you'll get your job back, though."

"I'm not sure I want it back."

She was very aware of his arm sliding across the back of the couch behind her as he moved a little closer. She looked up at him, eager for this moment, but fearful. She had imagined it so many times, but it was a thousand times more intense in its reality. The desire in his eyes, the tenderness of his touch.

He was going to kiss her, she knew it. He brought his right hand up to lightly touch her cheek and very slowly leaned toward her, giving her plenty of time to pull away if she wanted.

Rebecca stopped breathing altogether. When his lips touched hers, she froze for an instant, but she couldn't stop her reaction. She returned his kiss hesitantly at first, then let herself slide her arms around him, receiving his comfortingly familiar embrace with joy and passion.

"Rob, I'm so sorry," she whispered in his ear. "Can you forgive me?"

He took two deep breaths before he answered. "Of course."

Rebecca closed her eyes as he bent to kiss her again and found herself wanting to hold him there forever. He was so warm and solid and real. His arms tightened around her as he lengthened the kiss.

She jerked away suddenly. She hadn't meant to cling to him so fiercely.

"I think you'd better go." It wasn't what she wanted to say, but her volatile reaction to his embrace had unnerved her, and she wasn't sure what would happen if he stayed any longer.

Rob sat very still. A hurt look had crept into his eyes. "Becca, please don't say that. It seems like you're always telling me to go away."

"I'm sorry. I didn't mean for good."

"No?" He took a quick breath.

"We have a date tomorrow, remember?"

He nodded gravely. "So, when you told me to leave just now, it wasn't like ... before?"

It pierced her heart to know he was carrying around so much pain, and that she had caused it.

"No, it's not a bit like that. I just think ... we need to say goodnight and continue this tomorrow."

His deep brown eyes were luminous when he met her gaze. "All right, I'll let you call the shots this time."

In spite of her words, she couldn't resist running her hand up the back of his neck, into his thick, soft hair, and he pulled her close once more. She closed her eyes again and rubbed her cheek softly against his scratchy jaw. Just the smell of him set her pulse racing, and she knew she needed to exercise caution. "Then I say you need to get out of here, and I mean fast. But come back in the morning."

He leaned back, and she peered up at him from beneath her eyelashes. He was looking at her uncertainly.

"Early in the morning," she added.

He smiled then and leaned forward to kiss her again, holding her tightly as if he would never let go, until Rebecca pushed him away with a gasp.

"You're still here," she choked.

"I'm leaving."

"Right." She turned her face away from him, but leaned against his shoulder, sighing deeply. Everything about him felt so right, she hated to let him go. Very gently he moved away from her and stood up.

"I'll see you. Go back to sleep." He pulled the blue afghan down off the back of the sofa and unfolded it over her.

Chapter 31

He came early, as promised, with Stewart and Connie and a complete breakfast. Connie had packed biscuits, sliced ham and homemade applesauce. Rebecca dusted off the coffee pot and started it brewing. She didn't dare think about the day ahead. So much had changed in the last forty-eight hours that she felt a bit on edge.

Nothing was said about the change in their relationship, but Rebecca caught Stewart and Connie smiling at her often, and everyone seemed extra happy in spite of the early hour.

"The pastor and a couple of other men from the church will be here soon," Stewart said over his second cup of coffee. "You two had better make your escape before they get here, or they'll try to put you to work stirring paint."

"Let me bring it in from the truck for you," Rob insisted. He made two trips to the pickup for the gallon cans, then asked his father, "Where do you want the ladder?"

"Would you just get out of here?" Stewart snapped. He winked at Rebecca. "Keep him away for a long time. I don't want him looking over my shoulder, telling me I missed a spot."

She laughed and ran upstairs for her sweatshirt. In the mirror she caught a glimpse of herself, through a film of dust. She was startled at the happiness in her face, despite the shadows beneath her eyes. *Thank you for this moment, Father,* she breathed.

Rob was at the dock when she went downstairs.

"Have fun," Connie called. Rebecca turned and waved, grinning, then raced down the path. Rob was arranging Connie's picnic basket and a quilt in the bottom of the canoe.

"What's in the basket?" she asked.

"Bait for bears."

"Your mom's the absolute best." She stepped down carefully into the canoe. Rob reached for her hand to steady her, and she let him help her without comment.

It was cool on the lake, with a definite tang of fall in the air. The maples and birches along the east shore were showing a bit of color.

Instead of going right to the island, they paddled down to the music camp. The campers were gone, and the beach was deserted. Rob took Rebecca's hand, and they walked over the grounds.

"You went to camp here, didn't you?" he asked.

"Yes, one season."

"Rebecca the flautist."

"If you've got it, flout it," she quipped.

"Ouch. That was painful. I remember you had a solo at the Christmas concert my senior year."

"Mm, *Winter Wonderland*," she said dreamily. "You took me skating afterward on the lake. Your dad made a bonfire, and half the kids from school came."

He slipped his arm around her waist and guided her toward the play area near the empty dining hall, where swings hung invitingly, swaying a little in the gentle breeze.

"Come on," Rob said. "I'll push you."

It had been years since she had swung, and Rebecca found the stomach-flipping soaring exhilarating. At last she cried, "Enough," and he let the swing slow, then went around in front of her and stopped it, holding the chains on each side of her.

"You want your contract now?" he asked, his voice husky.

"You brought it with you? What if we swamped the canoe?"

"Then I'd build a fire and dry it and you out."

She laughed. "All right, hand it over. Time for me to divest myself of all my property."

He unzipped his navy blue sweatshirt and took an envelope from the pocket of his shirt. "Here you go."

She glanced at the heading. It was from a law firm just down the street from Hanson Associates.

"Where do I sign this?"

"At the bottom."

"Do you have a pen?"

He took one from his inner pocket and handed it to her. She laid the paper on the seat of the swing, bending over it, her braid hanging down and brushing the paper as she began to write her name.

"Bec, you ought to read the fine print."

"Why? I know you did. I trust you."

He smiled and shook his head. "You'd be so easy to swindle." He folded the paper and put it and the pen back in his pocket. "Do you really trust me that much?"

"Shouldn't I?"

He seemed a bit disconcerted, and her mind jumped suddenly to the woman in the silver car.

"Rob, maybe we should clear the air about one other topic."

"You mean Brittany."

She felt suddenly chilled. He'd known immediately what she meant, and the woman's name slipped easily off his tongue. "I didn't—Well, I just ... Debbie said some things, and—"

"She shouldn't have."

"I asked."

"Oh."

"I asked her if you'd been seeing anyone, and she had to tell me. But she said you knew it wasn't right, that this woman was all wrong for you."

"That's true."

"That was in July."

"I'd ended it with her before Debbie stayed here with you."

"Really? Because Debbie seemed to think you were having a hard time making that decision."

He looked away, over the placid water, then back again. "I don't tell Debbie everything, but I'll tell you. I was stupid, and it's true I dragged my feet. Brittany got very upset every time I tried to bring up the subject. I felt like a heel, but when I got down to business with the Lord, I knew I had to tell Brittany right out in plain English that I didn't want to see her anymore. She didn't take it very well, but ... it's over. Completely."

She nodded, watching him cautiously, trying to gauge the depth of his regret.

"You still see her every day," she said softly.

"Not for long. She's accepted a job with a firm in Massachusetts. It's a good career move for her."

"You're not sorry she's leaving?"

"Not a bit. It's a huge relief, actually." He looked steadily into her eyes, and Rebecca didn't doubt his sincerity. "Becca, I'm so sorry I ever got involved with her. Can you forgive me?"

"Yes. Let's not talk about it again."

He nodded. "Look, if you change your mind later on and want to discuss it, I won't bark at you. I didn't love her. I just didn't want to hurt her feelings."

She let that sink in. "I don't blame her for being attracted to you." She decided it would be best not to tell him that she believed she had seen Brittany in all her beauty and self-confidence, and that she could understand the outward magnetism that had drawn him in.

Rob took a deep breath. "Come on, let's go to the island."

Her arms were aching by the time they beached the canoe again. Rob carried the basket and spread the quilt on the dry grass above the little beach. They could see the cottage across the expanse of water, tucked serenely between the big trees. Rebecca caught a whiff of wood smoke. She began setting out their lunch things.

"I'm starved." Rob reached for the package of cookies she pulled from the basket.

"Uh-uh, eat your sandwich first."

They greedily shared the lunch, like two children who'd been playing hard all morning. As she gathered up the empty dishes and wrappers, Rebecca felt a gentle tug on her braid.

She turned to face him expectantly, and he moved closer to her.

"Becca, I want you to stay."

Her pulse hammered, and she caught her breath. You're reading too much into this, she scolded herself. There were still things unsettled between them. She smiled cautiously. "I will. Until the thirtieth."

"But you'll need a place to stay after that. You let your apartment go."

"Yeah." She frowned and looked helplessly over toward the peaceful cottage. "I don't think I'm going back to Ainsley Hospital. But I can't stay here forever. I guess I should call my folks and hint that I'd like to come home for a while. They don't even know I'm up here."

"I told your dad yesterday."

"He called you?" She swiveled quickly to look at him, and his face was very close to hers. "Have they been trying to get hold of me?"

"No, I don't think so. He didn't call me. I called him."

"Oh."

He wrapped her braid carefully around his hand. "I needed to ask him something. I hope you don't mind. Maybe I should have asked you first."

She put her left hand on his chest to keep him from coming closer. She could feel his body heat through his sweatshirt, and she could smell him, that faint, masculine aroma that was Rob's smell. It made her want to fling herself into his arms.

"Becca." It was barely audible as his lips touched her earlobe.

She stiffened her wrist, holding him back. "What did you ask my father?"

He let go of her braid and touched her hair gently, stroking a few loose strands back behind her ear. "I asked him if I could court you again."

His formal phrasing told her how serious he was. She sighed and let her wrist go limp against his sweatshirt, leaning into his embrace, letting her forehead rest lightly against his collarbone. His other arm came around her and held her in comfortable closeness.

"My folks thought it was a good idea," he whispered.

"And what did my dad say?"

"He said, 'What took you so long?'" He kissed her neck, her jaw, and finally her lips. "I've loved you so long." His lips roved over her cheek and eyebrows, then he dropped a light kiss on the end of her nose. "So what do you think? May I call on you regularly, Miss Harding?"

She smiled, pushing away a little. "You mean our fathers haven't exchanged cattle and signed the contract in blood yet?"

"They're pretty eager. How many cows do you think your dad would ask for you?"

"Silly." She slid her right hand beneath his arm and settled in closer, resting with her head over his heart. She could hear it thumping rapidly.

"Stay at the cottage, Becca ... always."

He turned her face up toward him again, but she held up her hand, stopping him.

"Wait, we need to talk. Last night ... "

"What?" His eyes had a hint of the wounded look, and she hurried on.

"There's something I need to say. Things can't ever be right between us if I don't."

He looked out toward the lake, frowning, a touch of the old insecurity creeping back into his expression. "You're regretting last night?"

"No," she said quickly. "Not last night, just the last four years. I never told you that. I felt as if you'd quit caring, and I was wrong."

The fire came back into his eyes. "I never stopped loving you, Becca."

Her cheeks were wet with tears, but she ignored them, clinging to him vehemently. "It's taken me a very long time to realize that I was putting you ahead of God. When I needed comfort and support, I blamed you for not being there to give it to me. I wasn't depending on God for it."

He was silent for a moment, holding her close. "It wasn't all your fault. I've been blaming myself for neglecting you. You were right about that."

She took a deep breath. "I still love you, Rob."

"Does this mean you don't want me to go away again?"

"Never. Please don't ever leave me again."

"I won't." His arms tightened around her. "I'm sorry I made you so unhappy. I was so stressed at school, I thought I just needed to plow on through it, but somehow ... somehow I mixed up what was important with what was crucial. And the internship. I could have gotten by without that. But at the time, it seemed so important."

"It's okay," she whispered. "If you still love me, it doesn't matter anymore."

He kissed her again, and she knew her heart was his forever. She nestled against his shoulder, and he ran his hand the length of her braid.

"You've got to read the fine print, babe."

She straightened a little and stared at him in the sunlight, wondering if she'd heard correctly. "What?"

He shifted his weight and unzipped the sweatshirt, placing the folded contract in her hand.

"What did I sign?" she asked ominously.

He smiled but said nothing.

"How many cows, Rob?"

He chuckled and kissed her forehead. "I put the cottage in your name. It's your home now."

She unfolded the paper and skimmed the text quickly until she found it. "I can't pay you, Rob."

"Forget about that. It's my gift to you."

"But I—I can't make the payments."

"There aren't any. I paid off the mortgage yesterday."

She gasped. "You could do that? And you're just going to turn it over to me?"

"I had a faint hope that you'd let me visit once in a while."

She brushed back the hair that fell over his forehead and let her fingers caress the remnant of the cowlick. "I've missed you so much."

Rob put his hand to her cheek. "Will you marry me? I've waited so long, Becca. Please say yes."

She slipped her arms around his neck, smiling tremulously. "Yes."

The word seemed inadequate, but Rob pulled her close, hugging her tight. She was warm clear through with the knowledge that he hadn't changed, and his love was as constant as she'd wished it to be.

"Come on," she whispered after a moment. "Let's paddle over and tell your folks."

They carried the picnic things to the canoe and launched it. As they paddled across the lake, Rebecca forgot her aching muscles and let her eyes feast on her new home, the tiny cottage she loved so much.

"Better let me break it to the folks," Rob said as they entered the porch. "Mom will probably cry. Then she'll hint about wanting grandchildren right away."

Rebecca flushed as she set the picnic basket on the table. "Would that be so bad?"

"No, I guess I've been wanting a family of my own for a long while," he admitted.

She looked around. "Even with the renovations, this is an awfully small house for a family."

"I—I want to add on. I've drawn some plans. If you want that. I mean, it *is* your place now. But I was thinking a laundry room and a couple more bedrooms, and maybe a den."

She rested her head on his shoulder and closed her eyes as he squeezed her. "I'd like that. Remember that dream house of ours? The one we were going to build when you were making big bucks?"

"Yeah."

She smiled up at him. "I think this is it. I've never been happier than I am here. I just want to stay here with you forever."

THE END

About the author

Susan Page Davis is the author of more than one hundred published novels. She's a two-time winner of the Inspirational Readers' Choice Award and the Will Rogers Medallion, and also a winner of the Carol Award and a finalist in the WILLA Literary Awards. A Maine native, she now lives in Kentucky. Visit her website at: https://susanpagedavis.com, where you can see all her books, sign up for her occasional newsletter, and read fun features on her "Freebies" tab. If you liked this book, please consider writing a review and posting it on Amazon, Goodreads, or the venue of your choice.

Find Susan at:
Website: https://susanpagedavis.com
Amazon: https://www.amazon.com/Susan-Page-Davis/e/B001IR1CGA
BookBub: https://www.bookbub.com/authors/susan-page-davis
Twitter: @SusanPageDavis
Facebook: https://www.facebook.com/susanpagedavisauthor

More of Susan's Novels you might enjoy:

Mystery and Romantic Suspense:

True Blue Mysteries:
   Blue Plate Special
   Ice Cold Blue
   Persian Blue Puzzle
Skirmish Cove Mysteries
   Cliffhanger
   The Plot Thickens (releases October 2022)
The Maine Justice series:
   The Priority Unit
   Fort Point
   Found Art
   Heartbreaker Hero
   The House Next Door
   The Labor Day Challenge
   Ransom of the Heart
The Saboteur
The Frasier Island Series:
   Frasier Island
   Finding Marie
   Inside Story
Just Cause
You Shouldn't Have
On a Killer's Trail
Hearts in the Crosshairs
What a Picture's Worth
The Mainely Mysteries Series (coauthored by Susan's daughter, Megan Elaine Davis):
   Homicide at Blue Heron Lake
   Treasure at Blue Heron Lake
   Impostors at Blue Heron Lake
Trail to Justice
Alaska Weddings Series:

Always Ready
Fire and Ice
Polar Opposites
Tearoom Mysteries (from Guideposts, books written by several authors):
Tearoom for Two
Trouble Brewing
Steeped in Secrets
Beneath the Surface
Tea and Promises
Tea Leaves and Legacies

Also from Guideposts, selected books by Susan appear in the Patchwork Mysteries, Mysteries of Mary's Bookshop, Miracles of Marble Cove, Secrets of the Blue Hill Library, and Mysteries of Silver Peak series.

Short Story Collection:
Short and Sweet: 13 Sweet, Romantic Stories

Historical novels:

Homeward Trails Series:
The Rancher's Legacy
The Corporal's Codebook
The Sister's Search
The Outlaw Takes a Bride (western)
Counterfeit Captive
Almost Arizona
River Rest (set in 1918)
The Crimson Cipher (set in 1915)
Mrs. Mayberry Meets Her Match
Hearts of Oak Series (Co-authored with Susan's son James S. Davis, set in the 1850s):
The Seafaring Women of the Vera B.
The Scottish Lass
The Ladies' Shooting Club Series (westerns):

The Sheriff's Surrender
The Gunsmith's Gallantry
The Blacksmith's Bravery
Captive Trail (western)
Cowgirl Trail (western)
Hearts in Pursuit (western novella)
Christmas Next Door
Echo Canyon
The Prairie Dreams series (set in the 1850s):
    The Lady's Maid
    Lady Anne's Quest
    A Lady in the Making
Maine Brides series (set in 1720, 1820, and 1895):
    The Prisoner's Wife
    The Castaway's Bride
    The Lumberjack's Lady
Seven Brides for Seven Texans
Seven Brides for Seven Texas Rangers
White Mountain Brides series (set in the 1690's in New Hampshire)
Wyoming Brides series (set in 1850s):
    Protecting Amy
    The Oregon Escort
    Wyoming Hoofbeats
The Island Bride (set in the 1850s)

And many more! **See all of her books** at
https://susanpagedavis.com.
Sign up for Susan's occasional newsletter at
https://madmimi.com/signups/118177/join